"I . . . I THINK I'M GOING TO KISS YOU . . ."

His voice was low. "When will you know for sure?"

She didn't reply; her breath was caught in her throat. There was the slightest pressure on her spine as Ben drew her closer. Without another word, they wrapped their arms around each other and began to kiss.

The actions of Ben's pliant mouth were triggering an exquisite yearning inside Jennifer. The feather-light movements of his fingers sent a shudder through her frame. The yearning that flowed between them was quickly dissolving into a compelling rush of physical excitement, and Jennifer found that she could only surrender totally to this joyous ecstasy . . .

LESLIE MORGAN was raised in a small Minnesota farming town. As she says, "I began writing as soon as I learned the alphabet because there are no diversions in a prairie town except identifying pickup makes." She earned a B.A. in journalism at the University of Minnesota and has worked in public relations and as a legislative aide.

Dear Reader:

The editors of Rapture Romance have only one thing to say—thank you! At a time when there are so many books to choose from, you have welcomed ours with open arms, trying new authors, coming back again and again, and writing to us of your enthusiasm. Frankly, we're thrilled!

In fact, the response has been so great that we now feel confident that you are ready for more stories which explore all the possibilities that exist when today's men and women fall in love. We are proud to announce that we will now be publishing six titles each month, because you've told us that four Rapture Romances simply aren't enough. Of course, we won't substitute quantity for quality! We will continue to select only the finest of sensual love stories, stories in which the passionate physical expression of love is the glorious culmination of the entire experience of falling in love.

And please keep writing to us! We love to hear from our readers, and we take your comments and opinions seriously. If you have a few minutes, we would appreciate your filling out the questionnaire at the back of this book, or feel free to write us at the address below. Some of our readers have asked how they can write to their favorite authors, and we applaud their thoughtfulness. Writers need to hear from their fans, and while we cannot give out addresses, we are more than happy to forward any mail.

Happy reading!

Robin Grunder
Rapture Romance
New American Library
1633 Broadway
New York, NY 10019

AGAINST ALL ODDS

by
Leslie Morgan

PUBLISHER'S NOTE

This novel is a work of fiction. Names, characters, places, and incidents are either the product of the author's imagination or are used fictitiously, and any resemblance to actual persons, living or dead, events, or locales is entirely coincidental.

NAL BOOKS ARE AVAILABLE AT QUANTITY DISCOUNTS
WHEN USED TO PROMOTE PRODUCTS OR SERVICES.
FOR INFORMATION PLEASE WRITE TO PREMIUM MARKETING DIVISION,
THE NEW AMERICAN LIBRARY, INC., 1633 BROADWAY,
NEW YORK, NEW YORK 10019.

Copyright © 1983 by Leslie Morgan

All rights reserved

SIGNET, SIGNET CLASSIC, MENTOR, PLUME, MERIDIAN and NAL BOOKS are published by The New American Library, Inc., 1633 Broadway, New York, New York 10019

First Printing, November, 1983

1 2 3 4 5 6 7 8 9

PRINTED IN THE UNITED STATES OF AMERICA

*This book is dedicated
with love and thanks
to my parents.*

AGAINST ALL ODDS

Chapter One

It was seven o'clock in the morning and still dark when Jennifer Aldrich strode through the tall double doors of the St. Louis *Herald*. She traded nods with the front desk guard, who knew her on sight and headed for the main elevator.

When the elevator doors whooshed shut, Jennifer sagged a little. She wasn't drowsy—she usually bounded to work at this hour—but all was not right this morning. She was feeling a faint sting of sadness, because of a man—or men in general. She wasn't sure which. She didn't want to think about it.

She got out on the fourth floor, which housed the editorial offices, the newspaper's inner sanctum. In the dim light, the blue and gold offices appeared spacious, sleek and clean. When the fluorescent overheads were flipped on, they would reveal how thoroughly lived-in the newspaper offices really were, with coffee stains and cigarette burns scattered all over desktops and the beige carpet.

Jennifer hung up her navy reefer coat before plucking the first edition of the morning *Herald* from a pile on the receptionist's desk. Automatically she flipped to the editorial page while walking unseeingly to her cubicle in the editorial/opinion suite. Turning on the architect's lamp, she perched herself at a drawing board. Outside her window the distant yet unmistakable shape of the Gateway Arch was catching the first rays of the cold winter sun.

The first thing Jennifer always looked for in the morning was the political cartoon. She had been the *Herald*'s editorial cartoonist for a full year now. At age twenty-seven, she was a successful young woman in an older man's field. Her work was regularly syndicated by a national service and occasionally appeared in the weekly news magazines. The exposure was par for the course for any talented political cartoonist, so Jennifer was fairly anonymous within her ranks.

Her air was efficient, aware and modest; her look was pretty and chic in a carefree, natural way. Jennifer was just under average height, her body lissome and well proportioned. Her hair was of the darkest auburn brown, a deep mink color, worn in a cap of wayward curls. Her features were as clear and alive as her sharply etched drawings: the small mouth and nose were tilted upward, and her brown eyes were enormous and sparkly. Today Jennifer's coloring was enhanced by the chocolate-colored wool dress she'd worn as a defense against the Missouri January.

"Very funny, Aldrich. Very good."

With a small start Jennifer looked over her drawing table at Lynn Fantle-Johnson, a government reporter who liked to get to work as early as she did. Lynn held a copy of the paper folded open to her cartoon. "Thank you," Jennifer replied modestly. "I like to think it hit the nail on the head."

For a moment they both gazed at her caricature.

Two days earlier the governor's wife, ex-New Yorker, Alva Jacobson, had announced she'd "love to start a foundation to benefit the poor hillbillies of the Ozarks." Her comment was absurdly misguided. In response, Jennifer had sketched Mrs. Jacobson as "Alvita," a Lady Bountiful in the Eva Peron mold, extending her arms to astonished moonshiners. Jennifer was so skillful with pen and ink that with two or three faint lines she had conveyed the subtle but telling nuances required for her scenario: startled apprehension on the moonshiners' faces, self-righteous magnanimity for Alva Jacobson.

"What have you got in this morning?" she asked Lynn while turning to the paper's front section.

Lynn slouched elegantly into a gold vinyl office chair, answering, "Not much, just an analysis of a federal agriculture bill that might interest a few farmers in northern Missouri."

Accompanying Lynn's by-line was a photograph of youthful U.S. Congressman Benjamin Trostel, whose opinions on the bill were quoted in her article. Jennifer knew Ben Trostel was notorious for being a "glamour boy," a popular, intelligent politician with movie-star looks. His profile was clean, composed, even heroic. His expression was easy and personable.

Jennifer had drawn only one cartoon of him to date. He looked intriguing, but he was a lawmaker, so he only interested her professionally; she looked at him much as a scientist looks at a butterfly stuck with a pin and displayed on a board.

Jennifer asked Lynn, "Did you get to talk directly to Trostel for this story?"

"Yes, I tracked him down at a corporate lunch in town, right before deadline." Lynn sipped coffee from a Styrofoam cup. She was a black woman in her early thirties, and to Jennifer she resembled a living Modigliani, very tall and very thin. Her Missouri drawl was as aggressive as her bulldog like investigatory skills. She smiled and ruefully shook her head. "Honestly, Jenny, every time I see Trostel I'm reminded of the caricature you ran of him last month."

"I've never seen his comely mug in person. I've just had his photographs to go on."

"If you met him, you'd be surprised how accurate your 'How to Be a Young Turk' cartoon was. Those rules: 'Undo your tie five minutes after it's knotted; roll up your shirt-sleeves immediately upon purchase of shirt; mix earnest concern with the constant twinkle in the baby blues.' Everything rang true. You got Trostel's entire character down in one cartoon better than a ninety-inch personality piece would have."

"I'd love to meet him, if only to verify the accuracy of my drawings. Speaking of Trostel, how is Senator Baker doing? Have you heard yet this morning?"

"For an old man with galloping pneumonia, he's doing great as far as I know."

Missouri's Harris Baker, a stereotypical old-fashioned senator and a public figure for over thirty years, was practically a national landmark. He was also widely known as Ben Trostel's mentor and personal sponsor in Washington. Unfortunately, like many legendary leaders who are widely beloved, Baker was very old. After a long period of various lingering illnesses, he lay stricken in the hospital with pneumonia.

Lynn pushed the subject away from the political to the personal. "Say, didn't you have a date with Rick Lindbom at some three-star restaurant last night?"

Jennifer threw up her hands in disgust. "Lynn, I'm

giving up on men!" Her words came out in a gust of emotion.

"It's a little early in the morning to be giving up on anything, isn't it?"

"I'm definitely giving up on Rick, though he doesn't know it yet. I'm telling the receptionist that if he calls I'm not available. In every sense of the phrase."

"What brought this on?"

"I've been dating Rick for about six weeks. As you know, I enjoyed his company, though he's an engineer and not particularly interested in current events. But tell me"—Jennifer became vehement—"did you ever hear me say that I was interested in him in a permanent sense? That I dreamed about him? Did I ever pronounce his name like a *caress*?"

"No!"

"And never once do I think I implied to Rick that I wanted a full-blooded, all-out relationship, a commitment of any kind. But on our second date, he was telling me that he didn't want us to 'get serious.' Rick is thirty years old, mind you."

"I'd say that's a little long in the tooth for that kind of high school timidity," Lynn said sarcastically.

"We saw each other twice, maybe three times a week. I didn't ask him for more time. I never called him. But for some reason he would say little things like, 'You're too good to me.' Once I made the mistake of pointing at a cute baby and Rick said"—and here Jennifer deepened her voice to hypermasculinity—"'I don't like it when women look at kids that way.'"

Lynn burst out cackling. "He sounds like a real prince!"

"Believe me, except for that kind of talk he was all

right. A lot of fun. Interesting, even. Then last night, we were eating at The Willows. I commented that I was having a lovely time. Rick said, 'When women say they're having a good time with you, they always want something.' I should have walked out, but I was curious. I asked, 'Tell me, Rick, what *do* I want from you? I want to know.' He said, 'I'm not sure. You're a hard one to read.' "

Lynn laughed, then said, "When you introduced us, he acted as though he liked you very much."

"Maybe he did. Maybe he's feeling one thing and saying another." Jennifer sighed heavily. "If I were a writer instead of a cartoonist, I could write a book about his type—so afraid of getting close to a woman that they fight them even as they get romantically entangled." She stretched to take a sip from Lynn's coffee.

"If you never really cared about Rick, why are you so upset this morning?" Lynn probed.

Jennifer gazed out her window, and the soft gray light of morning bathed the contours of her face, emphasizing its wistful expression. Thoughtfully she replied, "I don't think I'm as upset with Rick as I am with what he *represents*. Rick stands for my lack of success with men, my poor 'track record.' "

"You've had plenty of boyfriends, Jenny. Maybe you've just ended things with them before they could develop."

"No . . . it's just that the men I've gone out with have all shown themselves to be men I can live without. Like Rick, they're running scared, terrified of assuming the responsibility of intimacy. Or they're chauvinistic and say my work is 'bitchy and catty' instead of incisive. Or they're intimidated by my position. I've dated jealous types, manipulators, hot-and-heavy Lotharios. They all seemed perfect—at the start." Jennifer's expression was suddenly somewhat bewildered. "Lynn, is there something about me that attracts these cads and cowards? Am I giving off the right signals to the wrong men? Worse yet, do I sound self-pitying?"

"Of course not, Jenny. But it's only natural that you haven't met a good man, the right man. If you had met that guy—and you will—you'd have married him already. You sound just like I did five years ago, before I met my husband."

"Ah, you really scored with David," Jennifer said, shifting in her swivel chair. "You got the last of his kind. He's good-hearted, open, solid. He listens when you talk. He makes a darn good friend as well as a good husband."

"David is not the last of an extinct species!" Lynn said with a laugh. "There are millions of men out there."

"Yeah, maybe even four or five good ones. I'm more than ready to be swept off my feet, Lynn. I want to meet someone who's mature, supportive, unafraid, someone who's got the ability to laugh at himself. I want to meet him *now*."

"I thought you just said you've had it with all men!"

Jennifer smirked. "Well, maybe there's *one* decent fellow lying in wait for me."

The reception area just outside Jennifer's door was abruptly flooded with fluorescent light. Lynn and Jennifer turned to see editorial editor Frank Quarters standing at the doorway. "Good morning," they chorused cheerily at the gruff old journalist who was never seen without his dapper bow tie.

"Haven't you two heard the bad news?" Frank asked in his gravel-rough voice. When the two women shook their heads, he stated, "Senator Harris Baker died a half hour ago."

Both Lynn and Jennifer were stricken, and their faces reflected their despair. Jennifer had met Baker only once, but even that was enough for her to fall under the spell of his forceful personality. Lynn had been on a first-name basis with the senator for years.

"I'm calling an editors' meeting in a half hour." Frank shook off his raincoat. "We don't have time to sit around and grieve. We have a memorial issue to put out."

The following day, as television news reports showed thousands of people waiting to file past Senator Baker's coffin in the U.S. Capitol rotunda, Frank Quarters and Jennifer were sequestered in his office, talking intently.

"For just a kid, Jenny, you do some damn fine work," Frank growled. He tapped on the morning *Herald* spread on his desk. It was open to the editorial/opinion page, which prominently displayed Jennifer's drawing of Mount Rushmore's four monumental faces weeping. The cartoon clearly honored Harris Baker, even though there was no caption.

Jennifer was long used to her editor's brusque way of complimenting her. She nodded. "Thanks."

"But we have to think about future issues while everyone else is still shook up by Baker's kicking the bucket—no one more than me. I'm going to miss that old buzzard," Frank said thoughtfully. With more force, he confidentially continued, "Now I've been told by a chum in Jefferson City that Governor Jacobson is going to appoint Mrs. Baker to fill her husband's seat till the general election this fall."

"Interested in a Madame Senator cartoon of some sort?" Jennifer watched Frank while he took his time lighting one of his pungent cigars. She thought her boss had the visage of a hound dog, except that his eyes were piercing and ironic. Quarters still lived in the era of hot type and "stop the presses!" He insisted on using a typewriter instead of a computer terminal, often declaring that he'd use a word processor when he wanted to "process words like a garbage disposer." Funny and encouraging, Frank inspired boundless devotion from his staff.

With the cigar safely lit and stuck between his teeth, he finally replied, "Nope. The issue coming up is who Baker's party really wants to run for his seat when his wife's time is through."

"It's going to be a big election year. Missouri has the governorship and both senatorial seats free."

"Who do you think the party is going to try to put in the Senate, Jenny?"

"One of the party's favorite sons, Ben Trostel."

"Right. Baker had his eye on him from the time Trostel was an eighteen-year-old freshman volunteer and had raised an incredible amount of money for one of Baker's campaigns. When he met Trostel and started talking to him, he immediately discerned that Ben was a young man with something extra. Baker initiated the traditional political grooming process then, and kept it up while Trostel got his bachelor's and law degrees. So Trostel's been under preparation for the throne for a good thirteen years."

"What do you think Trostel's chances are for becoming senator? Minimum eligibility is thirty. If he's only thirty-one, everyone's going to say his ears are too damp for the job."

"There won't be any problem. After spending just four years in the House, Trostel is catnip in this state. His philosophy is similar to Baker's, and his concern for the poor is undeniable. He's told me that what he wants from politics is a sense of promoting justice, of being useful to people."

Jennifer shrugged, unimpressed. "I've always perceived Trostel as a too-smooth whiz kid. You know, the hail-fellow-well-met type, a backslapper and hand pumper. Ambition for ambition's sake."

"Don't let that handsome face and the 'young Turk' image fool you. There isn't anyone in Congress who works as hard as he does. He's devoted to duty and honor. Since Trostel is such a winning combination of glamour and grit, he's practically a shoo-in for the Senate."

"How do we even know Trostel himself wants to be senator?"

"Even if he doesn't want to run for higher office, we can be sure his party wants him to." Frank puffed at his stogie, then pointed it at Jennifer. "Trostel can become this state's greatest political leader and spokesman within the next ten years, and his party isn't about to let a potential power figure like that slip through its fingers. Ben doesn't act politically hungry, as many politicos are, but his party's aspirations for him are plenty greedy."

"I'd better study up on Trostel. If what you're saying is true, I'm going to be doing a portfolio full of Senator Trostel cartoons over the next few years."

Frank nodded once. "As for our current situation, it's way too early for Lynn or any of the other government reporters to come up with an analysis of who's going to fill Senator Baker's shoes. Not until Dorothy Baker officially declares she's not running for the seat. However, we can jump the gun by offering a little pictorial representation of who's bound to be the heir to the throne. I'd like to run the cartoon the day after the funeral. Can you handle it?"

Jennifer paused, trying to come up with an idea on the spot. Then she gave the only answer Frank ever accepted from his staff: "Yes."

"Good. Why don't you mull it over?"

Jennifer knew she was being dismissed. She left Frank's office wondering how many cleansings would be needed to remove the overpowering cigar odor from her hair and clothes. She slowly walked back to her small office, lost in a cloud of heavy thought.

Darlene, the fiftyish receptionist with a too-blond ponytail and a lot of bosom, called, "You've got a message here, darlin'. From Rick Lindbom."

The name interrupted Jennifer's reverie. "I do?"

"Yeah, and I told him you weren't available." Darlene, who was on her fourth husband, gave an understanding wink. Jennifer grinned back, then went into her office to begin doodling.

Out of the corner of her eye she saw the glass and cement structures of St. Louis turn dark blue, then purple, then black scattered with a yellow lacing of office and apartment lights. As it grew later Lynn and a couple of other friends from the city room came to say good night or to compliment her on the day's cartoon. Darlene left after bringing Jennifer a last cup of black coffee.

Frank stopped in, belting his trench coat against

the miserable coldness he'd be stepping into momentarily. "Got an idea yet, kid?"

Jennifer tightened her lips. "I'm not sure." Her huge, engulfing eyes looked dull in the glow of the architect's lamp. "How about the ghost of Harris Baker wearing a track suit and passing a baton to Trostel, as if they're in some sort of relay?"

"Bad. Very bad."

"I know." Jennifer was humorously resigned.

"Almost as bad as something you'd see sketched on a grade school kid's desk."

"Hey! Some of the best cartoonists I know started out that way!" Jennifer protested, referring to herself.

"I'm confident you'll come up with a little number worthy of this year's Sigma Delta Chi Award. Or your first Pulitzer Prize. Right?" Frank shut off the reception area's overhead lights as he left.

When the right idea emerged from Jennifer's scratchings fifteen minutes later, it was so perfect that her heart skipped a beat.

The caption of this drawing would be "The Sword in the Stone." White-maned Harris Baker, looking spectral and deific, would be in the guise of Merlin the Magician. Ben Trostel, as the future King Arthur, would hold aloft the magic sword "Excalibur," which he would have just pulled from a stone labeled "Fall Elections."

Jennifer clipped photographs of the late senator and Trostel to the top of her drawing board and began to etch their figures in ink. She was careful to make her sketch look like a drawing instead of a cartoon to ensure its appropriateness to Baker's memory. Her first drawing of Trostel had been a caricature, but now, as she etched the lines of his portrait, she quickly discovered she was copying his face more naturalistically. For some reason, she began to feel strange as she did so.

He's too handsome for his own good, Jennifer decided. I don't think I'd trust an elected official who was this devastating-looking.

The photo in front of her showed a young man with a candid, relaxed face that was rather long in shape. His smile was a flash of white and there were long parentheses etched around his mouth. The hard lines of his face seemed imposed by the emotional and physical climate of the American West, not St. Louis. Jennifer couldn't make out the true color of the eyes from the black and white photograph, but they were definitely fringed with thick, long lashes. The hair, disheveled and a little overgrown, was dark blond or light brown. Trostel's overall look was striking, and disturbingly sensual.

"He probably gets the vote of every eligible female in his district," Jennifer muttered, annoyed at the way his photograph made her feel. Missouri had ten congressional delegates, and Trostel's district included a major hunk of St. Louis. As she sketched in a lush forest in the background of her picture she finally realized why it had felt so odd to copy Trostel's portrait. He was so attractive that carefully drawing his face felt almost as if she were stroking it, caressing it.

At that flash of insight, Jennifer finally knew that she was down for the count. I'm hallucinating, she thought. Time to go home. She scrawled her distinctive "J. Aldrich" in the corner of her drawing, then placed a call for a cab, not wanting to walk through the deserted streets to her downtown condominium.

The following morning while Jennifer was eating

breakfast, Frank called her and told her that the "Excalibur" drawing was just what he had wanted and to come in as late as she wished. She thanked him and crawled back into her large, ruffled bed to luxuriate.

Senator Harris Baker's funeral was on Monday. The following day her cartoon was published. The state chairman of Baker and Trostel's party called Frank Quarters with a mild protest. But then he chuckled sheepishly and coyly suggested that the *Herald* editorial staff "just might be accurate" in its cartooned prediction.

Late Thursday afternoon Jennifer sat at her slanted drawing table, sharpening her pencils and cleaning her paint box. She felt an extraordinary sense of well-being, maybe even a touch of smugness. The product of her satirist's pen had been of consistently excellent quality over the past two weeks. And she'd mostly forgotten about the Rick Lindbom debacle. Naturally she couldn't help but desperately wish she could find that one decent fellow she knew was out there somewhere waiting for her, but her current satisfaction in her work made that seem less urgent, at least for the moment.

Editors, reporters and technical people began to leave the fourth floor in a slow, continual stream as afternoon turned into the supper hour. Jennifer bade good night to Darlene while idly flipping through the pages of a political cartoonists' quarterly. She spread it over her drawing board. Bending her dark curly head over the magazine, she was quickly absorbed, totally unaware of anything but the pages in front of her.

She wasn't conscious of how long she'd been reading until a faint gray shadow glided into the yellow light of her lamp. Jennifer looked up, the smallest frown creasing her forehead, to see a very tall, extremely attractive man standing in front of her table. The immediate jolt of recognition that hit her nearly made her fall backward off her chair.

She couldn't help but stare at him. He was the very portrait of professional success, a man in effortless control of the situation. The blue, blue eyes were electric, honest, mischievous, haunting. They had a penetrating gaze that seemed to pierce her. None of these qualities had been apparent in his photograph.

He slowly extended his hand. "Jennifer Aldrich? I'm Ben Trostel."

Chapter Two

Jennifer rose unsteadily, then reached over her board for his firm handshake. His well-formed hands were supple despite their large size, the fingers long and graceful. "How do you do, Congressman," she murmured. Her head filled with a dizzy, expanding sensation, yet she managed to walk around her desk to stand face-to-face with him.

"No, not Congressman. Just Ben." She could feel his soft, deep voice reverberate right inside her own chest.

"It's sort of a shock to see one of your cartoon subjects in the flesh so unexpectedly," Jennifer said, looking into the bright sparkle of his eyes. They conveyed both a good-natured humor and solid assurance.

"I've visited the *Herald* offices enough times to feel comfortable walking in here," Ben said. Jennifer guessed he was nearly a full head taller than she. With his height, his striking looks and vitality, he couldn't help but dominate any room he entered. She tried to keep from staring at him. "I was in the vicinity and I came up on the slight chance the cartoonist would be here."

In person Trostel looked a little older than thirty-one. The subtle character lines on his face gave him the appearance of having stepped out of the Old West; he looked like a cowboy or a rugged plainsman who had spent many days in the sun, gazing through clouds of dust to the sun-streaked horizon. She was almost compelled to touch those lines, smooth them, just to see what he felt like.

From far away Jennifer heard him say, "I've always admired the work of Jennifer Aldrich, but I must say, I had no idea that that sharp-witted woman was so pretty." Jennifer laughed evasively. He seemed to be staring at her as well. "Or that she would be young and single."

"How do you know I'm single?"

Ben touched Jennifer's left hand fleetingly. "Your left hand looks awfully bare."

She imagined a slight mocking in his tone and her brown eyes narrowed slightly. "As is yours. Is there anything I can do for you?"

"Well," he started edgily, "I want to compliment you and ask you a favor both."

"You would like to say that the 'Excalibur' drawing we published Tuesday was great, and that you'd like the original to frame for your office."

His voice acquired a pleased tone. "How did you guess?"

"It's not unusual for a cartoonist's subjects to request the original drawing." Jennifer spoke cordially. "Some of us won't give the original away at any price, but there are others, like me, who consider it an honor to be framed on someone's wall instead of being filed away." Ben gazed down intently into her eyes. He touched his own finely carved lips as she spoke. "Be my guest, 'Excalibur' is all yours. It will come back from the composing room in a few days, and I'll get it to you as soon as I can."

Ben's face lit up. "Terrific. Thank you. I can't tell you how much this means to me. The drawing was right on the mark. Harris was often like my own private Merlin, showing me how to pull the sword out of the stone. Very flattering likeness, by the way."

"How are you feeling now?" she inquired with compassion. "I heard on the radio this morning that you were scheduled to speak at the memorial at Saint Paul's today."

Ben made a small grimace. "I met Harris Baker at about the time my own dad died, and he's been sort of a surrogate father ever since. But I'm sure he would rather have me out affirming his legacy than sitting around rending my garments. As I said today at the memorial service, the joy of Harris's memory and vision is going to outlast the sorrow of his leaving."

Jennifer was touched, and impressed. "Did you compose that eulogy yourself? Those words about the sorrow and the joy?" He gave a little nod and she said, "It's very nice."

Ben chuckled uncomfortably and looked toward the ceiling a moment, exposing a silky patch of hair where his collar was unbuttoned and the tie loosened. Studying him closely, she could almost feel the brush of his five-o'clock shadow against the soft curve of her palm.

"Between you and me," he explained in a slightly confessional tone, "I was destined to be a writer, not a politician." If he was destined to write, why was he working his way up as a public official? Jennifer was surprised, but remained silent as he continued. "I even earned my undergraduate degree in English way back in the dark ages before I became involved in politics and met Harris."

"Did you want to write fiction or—?"

"I've always been interested in nonfiction. Serious magazine articles, biographies. But never mind all that," Ben said suddenly, laughing somewhat self-consciously. "I've been remiss in my manners. I meant to drop in for a minute and I've been keeping you here, chattering about myself. You must want to go home, Jennifer."

She liked it that he called her Jennifer right away. Most people called her Jenny automatically. To her, a "jenny" was the name for a rickety old biplane.

"No problem," she replied. "I like to stick around the building when the day is over. I get more ideas here for some reason. The *Herald* is more inspiring than my condo." And much less lonely, she thought. "Plus it's a quick twenty-minute walk home. No buses to catch."

"Where is home?"

"The Crossings, the high rise at Fourth and Pine."

"We're neighbors. My pied-à-terre is at Ninth and Market. I'll go out of the way a little and walk you home."

Jennifer felt a fleeting anxiety. Ben Trostel's face and figure tempted her as someone she could adore. A single need echoed in her thoughts, but she was unsure of what the vague turbulence was. She rumpled her curls once and casually agreed. "All right. It will be nice."

She stepped away to retrieve her coat from the back of the office door. As she did so Ben's incredible blue eyes traveled admiringly over her lithe body, clad in rich herringbone-tweed pants and an olive turtleneck that outlined her breasts. Jennifer was very conscious of his gaze. She could almost feel the warmth of him, the vigorous energy he gave off. She slowly pulled on her reefer coat, dryly saying, "I notice your tie is unknotted, as usual."

Ben instantly caught her reference to the "Young Turk" caricature of him. His laughter erupted like bubbling water, a rich, full-bodied laugh. "I didn't like that particular cartoon at all! Not at the time, at any rate."

Under the distinctive greatcoat and gray flannel suit he was wearing, Jennifer could tell that his body was well muscled, but not thickly fleshed. What am I doing, she thought. Why was she thinking this way, so sexually? Never before, when she'd met a man, had she wondered what her sensual response to him would be. With Ben, she couldn't seem to think about anything else and it scared her.

When they emerged from the newspaper building, the crisp January air seared their lungs with its exhilarating coldness. They had a healthy twelve-block stroll through the heart of St. Louis before them.

Despite the cold, warm and vivid images kept playing around the edges of Jennifer's mind. The young representative was clearly as intrigued by her as she was by him. His direct, lingering glances told Jennifer at least that much. She had the distinct feeling that he'd like nothing better than to wrap one arm over her shoulders as they walked. They were the perfect heights and builds for such a cozy maneuver, and it felt unnatural for them to walk as they were, with empty space hovering between them like an abyss.

As they turned a corner to begin walking east toward the Mississippi, Jennifer asked matter-of-factly,

"Weren't you sent on some marvelous overseas junket recently? I think I recall reading something."

"Yes, five congressmen were sent to Nigeria as a trade delegation," Ben answered, smiling a little. "It was unforgettable. The only wrinkle in the mission came at a state dinner when we were served snake meat. Raw, puréed snake meat."

Jennifer's stomach did a flip-flop. "Snake meat? Did you even taste it?"

"Of course! Demands of diplomacy, protocol and all that. Only one of the many things I do for my country."

"What does snake tartare taste like?"

"Better than termites. I've had those, too."

Jennifer giggled in unabashed delight. My god, she thought, Ben had everything! Looks, position, personality, humor. He might be single, but he certainly couldn't be a man who was doing without.

The sidewalk was sprinkled with traces of a recent snowfall, and plowed snow sat on the curbs in mounds like small mountains. At one corner Jennifer began to slip precariously and Ben caught her arm with rock-steady quickness. He is *strong*, she thought, tossing a quick, searching look at his profile. His arm slid down so that their gloved fingers intertwined. As her hand fitted into his she felt a physical circuit of electricity running back and forth between them. Without drawing attention to the act, she moved her hand away.

Just when Jennifer had been complaining that there were no "real" men to be found, she was meeting one who appeared to fit precisely into that vague category. It would be so easy for her—for any woman—to fall for Ben Trostel.

Yet he was a dyed-in-the-wool politician, she told herself as they walked, popular with backslappers and drooling babies. He can assume that unpretentious, vote-getting charm of his on command. Or he's so well practiced at being constantly on stage that his personality and his apparent concern are nothing more than automatic responses. And he *must* be taken by some capable woman already. Jennifer tried telling herself all these things, but they didn't feel true, and they didn't matter.

They had reached the corner where Ben's apartment building stood. Because it was an overcast night, the clouds caught and reflected the city lights and cast an eerie, incandescent glow over the skyscrapers.

"Are you in a hurry to get home?" Ben asked. His distinctive voice wrapped around Jennifer like smoke from a campfire. She felt herself come fully under his influence. She shook her head slightly and he added, "Would you like to come upstairs for a drink?"

"You don't have a constituent meeting or some dinner to attend tonight?"

"No, I've made myself unavailable for a while."

Jennifer looked at him steadily. Steam clouds of their breath mingled in the air between them. She heard herself respond, "Yes, I'd like to have that drink. But I can't stay long."

The ride in the elevator was silent. Jennifer couldn't quite identify Ben's cologne, but for some reason it made her wonder what he might taste like. She glanced at his upturned face and saw that while his eyebrows and hair were the same rich color, his eyelashes were coal black. Just as he returned her glance the doors whooshed open and they got off at the twentieth floor. Ben led Jennifer down the plain corridor, unlocked a door and let her inside. In the engulfing darkness he said, "Before I turn on the light, I must warn you not to be shocked by the unlived-in look of this place."

The hall light came on, and Jennifer instantly saw that they were in an efficiency apartment. The spartan living-room area looked as impersonal as a model apartment. There was a modular sofa and an easy chair covered in crushed caramel leather, a coffee table made of polished chrome and glass and a brass pharmacist's floor lamp. Nothing appeared to have ever been used.

"It looks like you've just moved in," Jennifer commented with surprise. She saw that the hallway led to an empty-looking kitchen area and a small dining room containing a desk.

"I have never really lived here," Ben answered, moving beyond her to switch on the living-room floor lamp. "I moved into this building two years ago, because it's in the heart of my legislative district. But I've been in town only twenty-five times in the last year, and I seldom bring people up. It's little more than a hotel, really."

They moved into the antiseptically white kitchen. Jennifer, marveling at how at home she felt in Ben's barren little space, asked, "What's your Washington residence like?"

"It's nearly identical to this cog-in-a-wheel layout, but it's cluttered up with books and papers. I have an apartment in the Watergate Hotel." Ben opened the refrigerator and added, "There's more food in my D.C. place, too. Bar's open."

The only items standing in the light of the appliance bulb were an unopened bottle of vodka and a pitcher of orange juice. "Don't worry, the orange juice is fresh. I fixed it last night. You can have any cocktail you like as long as it's a screwdriver. There's a tin of sardines somewhere around here, I think."

"Uh, I'll pass. Just a couple of drops of vodka with the O.J., please." Jennifer's expression reflected her amusement at his stereotypical commuting-bachelor's understocked larder.

Ben handed her a heavy whiskey glass. He turned off the kitchen light and guided her toward the living room. In the gold rays of the lamp his blue eyes glimmered. She wondered when, and if, he would make a pass at her. He reached to pull open the transparent white curtains, and the wall-sized window revealed a fantastic view of varicolored lights emanating from St. Louis's grand and dramatic skyline.

Jennifer ensconced herself in one of the cushiony leather armchairs. Ben remained standing a moment, looking out on the city. His face, suffused with light from the outside, was grim and unreadable. His shoulders were a little slumped, and suddenly Jennifer realized the hollowness he must have been feeling all week after his great mentor's death and how burdensome the Baker legacy must feel to him.

Quickly she mentioned, "What an incredible view you've got here. Almost the whole city in all its glory."

"Too bad I'm not here enough to appreciate the scenery." Ben turned around and dropped into a seat in the shadows opposite Jennifer. She was disappointed at being unable to enjoy his fine looks, but now she could scent his clean-smelling after-shave. He smelled of winter in the Rockies: fresh air, green pine needles, newly fallen snow. She found it very pleasing.

"Are you a St. Louis native?" she asked.

"Sure, I was raised here. How about you?"

"I grew up in a wide spot in the road in Indiana.

Maybe you've heard its name in American history—Tippecanoe? As in 'Battle of'?"

Ben again let out his unique laugh. " 'Tippecanoe and Tyler Too!' Sure, the campaign slogan of William Harrison, the president who died a month after taking the oath of office. Tell me, how does a slip of a girl from Tippecanoe get to the editorial offices of a major newspaper?"

"I've told this little story quite a few times," Jennifer said, shifting in her chair, "so I hope I don't sound like a tape recording. When I was a kid, I was interested in the political cartoons reproduced in my parents' magazines. For some reason they provoked me to draw 'funny pictures' too. My friends loved it when I did these crude but accurate little caricatures of our more despicable teachers. When I started reading those magazines instead of skimming them, I acquired a healthy skepticism about politics and the processes of government."

"When *I* started reading those magazines, *I* acquired a healthy respect for politics," came Ben's rich voice through the dimness. Jennifer felt a quick, illogical wave of affection and arousal. There was such a delicate mood between them. Anything could happen.

Calmly she continued relating that in her freshman year at Northwestern University, the huge student newspaper was hunting for a campus editorial artist. Jennifer quickly put together some sample cartoons and submitted them, mostly as a lark. Much to her surprise she was chosen. After she completed her degree in history, the daily newspaper in Lincoln, Nebraska, hired her as its editorial cartoonist. A syndicate put her under contract and her cartoons began appearing in an increasing number of publications.

The previous January the St. Louis *Herald*'s cartoonist announced his retirement. Jennifer applied for the position, won it and promptly moved to the river city.

She and Ben sat talking quietly, comparing their backgrounds, their educations, and lightly discussing their political philosophies. After the phone rang several times, Ben turned off its distracting bell. They talked about the origins of jazz, "The St. Louis Blues" and the St. Louis Blues hockey team. Jennifer felt completely at ease with him. She was talking about herself rather openly, considering she'd just met him. Ben seemed so much like herself that she couldn't help marveling over the fact.

At last it came to her: she was being made love to from across the room, and by a politician. A very handsome, sexy one at that.

She was roused from her ambling thought by his voice. "I thought you said you couldn't stay long."

"It's never wise to sound like your time is readily available." Her tone was humorous, and though she didn't mean it to sound that way, mildly suggestive.

Ben leaned forward into the lamplight, revealing a wide, delighted smile. His amused eyes looked boldly into hers, and she could feel her face become flushed and eager.

"I can't remember the last time a beautiful woman cared enough to manipulate me just a little."

They sat leaning toward one another in momentary, provocative silence. A pleasurable tension crept into the air.

"My glass is empty," Ben remarked.

He made a movement to stand, and Jennifer put up her palm to stay him. "Let me refresh your drink."

She rose, brushing nervously at the front of her

pants. As she started to walk past Ben's chair she felt his hand close tightly around her wrist in a no-nonsense challenge. A small *frisson* of surprised desire shot through her. She looked down at his eloquent expression, and a delicate peach color bloomed over her small face.

He tugged gently at her arm. She felt a moment of resistance, then she willingly sank into his lap as though it were the most natural place in the world for her to settle. Cradled comfortably in the warmth of his chest and arms, she could feel his muscular strength held in check within the gray flannel.

Their gaze flickered over each other. He was so good-looking. His face was impossibly sexy and intelligent at the same time. Jennifer's palm tentatively traveled up under his jacket lapel, detecting the broad, flaring shoulder bones hidden there. She could just barely feel his breath.

"You've got three dimples," Ben said slowly. "Here, here . . . and here." He went on, brushing Jennifer's cheeks and chin in sequence. His feather-light touches made her shiver undetectably.

Their lips were very close, their foreheads nearly touching. Jennifer let out a shuddering sigh. "I . . . I think I'm going to kiss you," she breathed, her color mounting.

Ben's voice was low. "When will you know for sure?"

She didn't reply; her breath was caught in her throat. There was the slightest pressure on her spine as Ben's large hand firmly impelled her closer. She kissed him timidly, and noticed that her uptilted lips seemed to fit perfectly against his mouth. They continued kissing with a measure of curiosity, then with more assertive mutual exploration. Jennifer, who was more than a little nervous, took her time savoring Ben's inviting lips. They were warm, moist and promised much pleasure.

She drew back slightly to regard the tan and blue tenderness of his face. His smile could have melted snowcaps.

Without another word they wrapped their arms around each other and began kissing in earnest. Jennifer's lips opened a little, and his tongue slid into her mouth, probing and circling, an action she returned with sweet longing. His kiss was almost rough, a little forceful. The edges of his hands lingered at the bottom of her full breasts. Yet it was clear he was not going to push her any further than she wanted to go.

Jennifer had always wanted to be kissed this way, with such wholeness of feeling and enjoyment, to be held in a strong, secure grasp just like this, and she had never known it. The simplicity and the exquisite happiness of this unexpected rapture astonished her.

His tongue traced her lips, forming an exquisite circle of fire over her mouth. The yearning that flowed between them was quickly dissolving into a compelling rush of physical excitement. Their simple embrace took on a strangely innocent eroticism.

Then Jennifer's palms pushed lightly against Ben's chest. She sat slackly on his warm thighs, her chin lowered. Ben leaned to kiss her throat just under the earlobe, then sat back, holding her. They listened to the sound of each other's deep and even breathing. Suspended. Jennifer knew he was waiting.

Deep inside her, right at her core, she felt a tiny new heartbeat. It had never sounded before. The sensation meant that Ben was the one Jennifer had always been wishing for, that she'd finally discovered him. He'd awakened a new entity inside her.

The feeling did not make her joyous, though, for as this new feeling pulsed inside her, a logical chain of thoughts marched through her head. She was frightened by her own physical want. A desire this sharp and intense couldn't possibly be good, or lead her the right way.

Jennifer's head snapped up abruptly and she stared at Ben so intensely that her eyes turned a full shade darker, to black. Ben's own eyes reflected his startlement at her expression.

I could love you, she told him mentally, her eyes narrowing with a taut guardedness. But the kind of love I would feel for you would only damage me. To love you would be to give of myself so completely, I don't know what would be left. If you were to leave me, I could not endure the depth of the sadness.

And there was more. Reluctantly Jennifer broke from the embrace and stood up, ruffling her hair. A troubled expression had descended over her face. It was all so right, and in a different way, completely wrong for a reason that had nothing to do with them. Did she have the strength to bring up the last problem that symbolically hovered between them like a specter from Pandora's Box?

Ben looked mystified by her abrupt withdrawal. His arms were held at an awkward angle, as though waiting for her to melt back into them.

She sighed. "Ben, we can't do this. I shouldn't even have come up here." Her desire still simmered inside her chest, and she tried to ignore it.

After a pause Ben said, "I think I know what you're going to tell me. That you and I are in two of the few remaining professions in life between which fraternization is an absolute taboo. That Hollywood would call us 'bad casting.'"

"Yes. You're a public figure, I'm on a newspaper. I have the dubious honor of interpreting your actions for the public's judgment." Jennifer pivoted and jammed her fists into her pockets, her eyes smoldering. "Journalism has strict, almost ancient codes of honor, Ben. Scrupulous objectivity is part of the job. I have to remain completely fair-minded toward all the people I handle in my work. And I have to remain emotionally uninfluenced by you at all costs! What we're doing right now is, for anyone on a newspaper at least, a crime against nature."

Ben's tone was delicately mocking. "Don't you think it's a little late for you to begin a lecture on objectivity? Let's face it, Jennifer, we've already passed the point of no return. There's no going back."

"You're right," Jennifer conceded resignedly, sighing.

"And *you're* right." Ben stood, loosened his tie and crossed the carpeted floor to put his arms loosely around Jennifer. She shifted her weight so that the top of her head fit right under his chiseled nose. "I know about these things," he said into her mink-brown hair. "I was in journalism once."

"You were?"

"Sure, when I was eight. I stood on a downtown street corner and sold the *Herald*. Or rather, I forced it on people. I banged on their car windows with my fist and shouted, 'You need this.' I sold papers like crazy.

"Seriously, I know it's forbidden for editorialists to socialize with the people they comment on, to ensure they're not personally prejudiced one way or the other

But in this case . . . ." He paused so long that Jennifer looked up at him searchingly. "It wouldn't hurt for us to see each other on a casual date, would it? After all, I have to be back in Washington soon."

"Well . . ." Jennifer hesitated. What would St. Louis's own late, great Joseph Pultizer say? What would the forbidding Frank Quarters say?

A lock of Ben's thick, fawn-colored hair had tumbled down over his high, cool-looking forehead. Jennifer was tempted to smooth it back, but it looked as perfectly disheveled as a model's in a cigarette ad, so she stopped herself. Her reservoir of opposition was draining rapidly.

"Yes, I'd love to see you," she murmured, telling herself that one or two dates couldn't hurt. I'll make myself forget about him as soon as he's back in Washington, where he's probably got a fiancée, or half a dozen of them. "I've got the weekend free. But first, didn't you offer to walk me all the way home before I allowed myself to be delayed?"

They had a cheerful walk of another seven or so blocks. They stopped, arm in arm, in front of a blue glass-and-steel building with a magnificent canopy. Jennifer turned to Ben, her face tingling with the cold. By now she was feeling almost safe with him.

"Thanks for the escort home, and thank you for the drink. It's been—" He stood there, looking at her fondly and cryptically at once. Desire suddenly choked her with a frighteningly compelling force. She quickly strained upward to kiss him, and a moan rumbled involuntarily from the base of her throat.

They drew apart, not taking their eyes off each other.

"You haven't told me when you're available for dinner," Ben said.

"Tomorrow."

"What do you think about lunch as well?"

"Lunch and dinner, both?"

Ben traced the impertinent line of her jaw with gloved fingers. "I have a healthy appetite."

Chapter Three

Jennifer sighted Ben as soon as she walked into the restaurant on the Mississippi River levee. Her heart fluttered with gladness. He was standing tall at the riverboat-shaped bar, wearing a down vest over an alpaca cable crewneck sweater that made him look more like a well-off ski bum than a U.S. congressman. Though he had seemed perfectly at home in his crisp suit the previous night, he looked more at ease in ranch-hand-chic duds.

Ben greeted her with a joyful kiss and a crushing hug. "You look great," he exclaimed as they sat down at a small linen-draped table.

"Thanks," Jennifer replied, trying to disguise her ridiculously boundless happiness at seeing him again. She had on a rat-catcher blouse with deep French cuffs and beige doeskin trousers. Breathlessly she asked, "What have you been doing this morning?"

"Not a lot. I called my office in Washington and told my secretary I won't be back till Sunday." Ben gave a sigh. "Do you realize I'm in my fourth session of Congress and I haven't missed a vote yet? But this last week, with Harris's funeral and my party's back-room discussions on a new senator, then meeting you, Jennifer"—his eyes sparkled with their open secret—"I figured I was entitled to play a little hookey."

"Feeling a dent in your dedication to the job, Congressman?" Jennifer's smile was provocative.

"No, just a little rebellion at having to be accountable to my constituents and party regulars for every day I live," Ben responded lightly.

As they gave their drink orders to the waitress Jennifer saw how other women in the restaurant seemed constantly to cast little admiring glances at Ben. Not once did he return them. His full attention was on Jennifer.

Even though the restaurant was filled to capacity, Jennifer noticed that Ben had been ushered to an excellent table as soon as she arrived. They were at the trendiest eating establishment in Laclede's Landing, a cobblestoned old-world river port that had been revived as a bustling commercial district. Jennifer wondered how many people in the exposed-brick and plant-scattered room recognized him as their Congressman Trostel, or how many people thought that the lean, striking man sitting opposite her looked vaguely familiar. Jennifer shuddered suddenly at the idea of people being able to recognize her on sight. She was intensely private, though her job was to lampoon public figures who were misguided or offensive. Ben was one of those figures, a minor celebrity who required public recognition and the media to keep his job.

Ben's deep, melodic voice interrupted her reverie. "I was halfway hoping that you slept very poorly after our meeting last night, but you look well rested."

Jennifer met the challenge that shimmered in his

Wedgwood-blue eyes. "No, I slept like a top for the first night in weeks."

"How fortunate for you. I tossed and turned in my lumpy little hide-a-bed." Ben's tone made her wish she could have witnessed this minor torment in person. "And what did you do this morning? You've got me curious; how does a political cartoonist go about getting those wild ideas?"

"I always get up pretty early, so I can meet my syndicate's deadline. On a typical day I come in, sit around a lot at my office and read newspapers and magazines from all over. Sometimes I bounce ideas off people in the city room or the editors."

"How many newspapers are your cartoons sent to?" She told him one hundred seventy-five, and Ben gave a low whistle. "How many of them do you turn out in a week?"

"Five. The syndicate doesn't use all of them, of course."

"I am impressed, very impressed," Ben said softly, his eyes intent on her. "But you're rather exciting as is, Jennifer."

She felt her color mounting uncomfortably, and she took a hurried sip of her champagne mimosa. "How's that?"

"For one thing, you're a very beautiful woman."

They both sat a moment with glasses poised and heads inclined toward one another, sharing a meaningful smile. Then their waitress came up behind them, addressing Ben as "Representative Trostel." As Ben ordered their eggs benedict, Jennifer blatantly studied his lightly tanned face. She was thrilled that he appeared to take so much interest in her work. Most men she had known talked solely about their own careers, never inquiring about Jennifer's unusual job. The thought struck her again: he is the one, the one intended for me.

The waitress slipped away. Ben turned back to Jennifer, rubbing his warm hand over hers for a fond moment. She briefly admired the sight of his rugged, golden flesh clasped over her own creamy, soft skin. He said, "Before we were interrupted, I wanted to ask you if you're as cynical as some of your cartoons are."

"Do I strike you personally as a bitter old skeptic?" Jennifer's voice was mock-wounded, but her smoky eyes revealed a small, real hurt.

"Not at all. In person you're sweet and mild-mannered, like Clark Kent." Ben flashed the half-abashed, half-knowing grin that had been reproduced in the St. Louis media over and over again. "But your drawings sometimes approach libel. You are very hard on the governor, the administration—all sorts of unfortunate pols."

With conviction Jennifer replied, "Only because they're hard on the public, Ben. Present company excepted, the politicians I meet invariably turn out to be vain, unctuous and unmovable in their personal visions. I've seen it! During a college interim I was a page in a state legislature. I learned then that elected officials on all levels think they're essential to the well-being of their poor, stupid constituents, that they're going to go down in history as charismatic, just leaders."

Ben ducked his head with an exaggerated grimace. "You're right, to some extent. Even the most talented, charming government leaders I've met have their days of foolishness and banality. Present company included."

"If I didn't let blood as nastily as I do, I'd be just another gag writer with a talent for drawing funny facial expressions." Her voice grew thoughtful, her tone measured. "It's not always easy, Ben. From time to time I've received hate mail that's far more malevolent than my cartoons. You can laugh it off, but when I publish a cartoon that genuinely *hurts* someone—that wounds their emotions rather than their political sensibility—it doesn't feel right."

Now Ben's hand came down over hers and stayed comfortingly. "It's always right to penetrate the image and show the truth, Jennifer," he said with a touch of urgency. "If you emphasize the provocative part of an issue, instead of making it amusing, you're bound to upset people. But you're also going to make them think. They'll read further into the problem you're illustrating. In the long run, you're going to benefit the figures you've satirized, not mortally wound them. If I ever get to sit down and do some writing again," he said as his eyes rolled briefly heavenward, "I'd like my words to be as powerful as *your* work."

Jennifer relaxed again. She greatly admired Ben for having just made her talk about the way she really felt about the disadvantages of her work, about what was important to her. She sat back in her chair and sighed. "We never expect any of the things that happen to us." She allowed her calf to extend and lean against Ben's. He pressed back, and the tingling warmth of his leg made her tremble imperceptibly.

His eyelids dropped knowingly, and Jennifer sensed that Ben knew of the exquisite longing his touch had sent through her. It was amazing how alone they could be together within the bustling restaurant. He casually asked, "When you were young, what did you want to have happen?"

"The usual."

"Which was?"

Jennifer smirked self-deprecatingly, though her brown eyes were warm. "Prince Charming. A pretty house with a green lawn and lace curtains. A gaggle of children who would wash their hands for dinner and say grace without prompting."

Ben smiled easily. "Everyone wants that. But I've never met anyone who's gotten it."

"No. I haven't gotten my Prince Charming," Jennifer replied. Could he tell what she was thinking as she looked at him? "But, as they say, I have kissed my share of toads!" Ben laughed, and she asked, "And you, what has your luck been?"

"With women? Fair to middling, I guess, for a man who's been as single as long as I have. I was engaged to a woman briefly about six years ago."

Jennifer felt the queer pinpricks of jealousy at her heart. "Can I ask what happened?"

"She was very likable, and that was about it. But my political cronies loved her, which helped me think I did too. The Bakers said she'd make the perfect political wife. It was only when she told me she'd help me get to the White House—the White House!—that I woke up and realized that I was marrying for convenience, not love."

Jennifer had been twirling the stem of her glass between her fingers, but now she stilled it. "You broke it off, then. How did your fiancée take it?"

"She was upset but not crushed. You see, her ambition was to be a politician's wife with all the rights and privileges thereof. She was more in love with a concept than with me, I think. It's not a pleasant story, and it doesn't reflect well on me, but I don't think it's a unique situation. Some politicians specifically want political spouses, and some people aspire to nothing less than to become one."

Ben shrugged and added, "I had to learn this through personal experience. Now I have definite ideas about what I want." Then, in a move that surprised and pleased Jennifer, he quickly leaned over the table to kiss her full on the lips and then sat back. The confessional interlude was over.

The mention of his writing ambition intrigued her, and she wanted to ask him about it, but just then their meal arrived. As Ben began to eat his entrée, Jennifer silently marveled over the way he made her feel that there was something exciting about her and that he was discovering exactly what that something was. He was so warm and funny and affectionate with her, despite their brief, if already impassioned, acquaintance. She never would have dreamed that this self-composed congressman, a target of her pen, would be propelling her to such romantic heights.

When Jennifer arrived at the *Herald* building an hour later, she found herself riding the elevator with Frank Quarters.

"What did you do for lunch?" he asked with genuine curiosity. "Your face is lit up like a Christmas tree."

"Oh, I just met a friend at Laclede's Landing." Before Frank could ask exactly who she had met, Jennifer went on, "There's such a breathtaking nip in the air outside! Really makes you feel alive. You should go for a walk. You'd love it."

Frank was unmoved. "I only love the fact that it's Friday."

At dinner that evening Ben and Jennifer sat talking for hours, as though they were starved for each other's company. Their conversation took place in a restaurant high atop a riverfront hotel. Once an hour the room made a complete revolution, offering the panorama of nighttime St. Louis from the Gateway Arch to the moored riverboats to Busch Stadium.

Jennifer was again amazed by their rapport, the effortless give-and-take of their exchanged confidences. Finally, when they noticed that they had sat through five revolutions of the dining room, Ben told Jennifer he was going to walk her home again. As they strolled through the empty streets a minor debate rattled in her head. Should she ask him up to her condominium for a drink? Or would that seem too forward, as though she wanted to complete what they'd started the night before? She was scared of feeling the same forceful need she had felt last night, the need for his complete touch.

She wanted Ben's company so much she was terrified of muffing everything. At this point she had to act the exact opposite of what she felt, right? In no way could she imply that she wanted an instant relationship, right?

But Jennifer found it hard to continue these high school ploys when Ben began kissing her within the Crossings' entryway. His mouth was deliciously inviting, its demanding caress over the full ripeness of her own lips soon leaving her light-headed. But she managed to step away graciously and accept Ben's offer to meet the following afternoon. He strode lankily out the glass doors, his blue eyes twinkling merrily.

Jennifer cursed herself as she entered the elevator. Why did she hang back from Ben when she wanted him upstairs with her? She had denied her true impulses, but she knew she had done so because she was afraid of her own want. She could fall in love with him so easily, make him the keystone of her world. That kind of fatal dependence was for other women, not for me, Jennifer staunchly insisted to herself.

Saturday afternoon turned out to be the best January day Jennifer had ever known in her life. She and Ben bundled up to walk through the streets of St. Charles, a charming historical district on the Missouri River that was once the home of Daniel Boone. White, fluffy snowflakes filtered down from the gray sky, gathering to muffle their steps over the brick-paved streets. The temperature was moderate and there was no wind, so they talked comfortably while looking over small town shops and houses that dated to the 1700s.

Ben dropped Jennifer off at her place at three o'clock, since he had a meeting of the "smoke-filled-back-room" variety to attend. He promised to return in several hours for dinner at her place.

Jennifer had decorated her spacious, one-bedroom apartment in restful earth colors and rich, natural textures. The living room was dominated by a rough stone fireplace, thick, handwoven Indian and sheepskin flokati rugs, a tan suede couch and multicolored candles everywhere. When she arrived home, she straightened out the room and then looked it over with satisfaction and anticipatory nervousness. What would happen here tonight, she wondered, sitting down for a minute of reflection.

Ben seemed so easygoing, so self-assured, a man of fine, relaxed determination. Yet under that nonchalant exterior, she sensed his core of exquisite and wild passion. Jennifer had perceived this in his unbridled and opulent kiss, his unrestrained curiosity and enjoyment in the simplest things. The sharp contrast between his golden composure and the sensual side of his nature excited, and challenged her. Challenged her to make him lose that composure, even at the cost of losing herself to him.

A massive florist's box arrived while she was tying on a wrap dress of body-hugging, crimson jersey. In the box lay twenty-four roses whose full-bloomed beauty was nearly heartbreaking. They were of an indefinable yellow-orange color. Enclosed with the fragant bouquet was the calling card of Representative Benjamin Trostel. He'd crossed off the "Representative," which amused Jennifer even as she was delighting in the flowers.

Ben showed up at her door wearing a plaid flannel shirt of slate blue and low-slung jeans that hugged the elegant lankiness of his legs. His cheeks were a robust pink from the cold outside, but his expression was sober. As soon as his eyes feasted on Jennifer, however, a light went on in his face.

"Very nice," he purred, placing his hands around her hips so they very nearly cupped her hindquarters. He stepped even closer, his eyes intimately inspecting her fluffy hair, her unnaturally excited, sparkling eyes, the curve of her tight-fitting dress. Then his gaze traveled around the room, which was intriguingly lit by a multitude of scented candles. Strains of Handel's "Water Music" floated from concealed speakers. "Very nice," he repeated, bringing his mouth close to Jennifer's. She could feel its moist warmth.

"I got your flowers," she whispered. "I've never seen anything so beautiful. Two dozen roses in the dead of winter—I simply don't know how to express my appreciation."

"I'm sure you can find a way." Ben was teasing, but

the look they exchanged left no doubt what was going on between them. His lips met hers with a kiss that was gentle and aggressive at the same time. One of his index fingers traced an erotic line down the buttons of her spine, sending a jolt of sensation through the jersey. Jennifer pulled back, suppressing a gasp at the abrupt desire that had taken hold of her.

"Sometimes you don't at all fit my idea of . . . of a congressman," she said limply.

"Oh please!" Ben protested, holding up a hand. "I'm off duty till tomorrow. Now what are you serving for dinner? I'm starved, Sunshine."

Taking Ben's hand, Jennifer led him to her teak dining-room table. "I hope you like sushi—you know, raw fish and rice? Is it too exotic for your taste?"

"Jennifer, you're a mind reader. Nearly every night I'm treated to another dubious entrée from the 'rubber-chicken circuit'; chicken or beef that's overcooked or underdone but always cold, served with a lump of vegetables or potatoes. You can't distinguish one lump from the other."

As Jennifer moved the bouquet of roses from the table to a credenza so they could see each other while eating, then laid out the large tray of artistically arranged sushi, Ben went on, "That's one of the hazards of being a legislator. Sometimes you receive up to thirty dinner invitations a week from constituent groups, and you don't know whose feathers you'll ruffle when you refuse them." His tone turned appreciative as he regarded his plate. "Honey, how did you make this? It's so beautiful it would be a shame to eat it. Mind you, the aesthetics won't stop me."

The platter between them held lumps of rice covered with tiny slabs of fresh raw fish—lobster, prawns, octopus, squid. Ben reached for a fork, rather than chopsticks, and took a shallow dish of the hot green Japanese horseradish paste endurable only by those with the staunchest of taste buds.

"Actually," Jennifer began carefully as she poured sparkling white wine into Ben's crystal goblet, "All I did was make a phone call."

"This is takeout food?"

Sitting down, Jennifer at last admitted, "I can't cook, Ben. I'm one of those helplessly undomestic women. Oh, I can fry and bake a couple of passable entrées, but nothing that would be good enough for an occasion like this."

Ben was amused by her confession. "I happen to be a gourmet TV-dinner cook myself. My mother calls me 'Harry K. Thaw from Pittsburgh.'"

Jennifer's affectionate laughter rose from her like the bubbles bursting in her glass. As she used chopsticks to dip some seaweed in her tiny bowl she moved to another subject. "You looked mildly disturbed when you arrived. Is anything the matter? Did something bad happen at the meeting?"

"No, not really. There was some shouting, a few arguments. Nothing out of the ordinary."

"Can you tell me? It's all off the record, of course."

Ben issued a heavy sigh. "Next week the governor is going to approach Dorothy Baker to formally request that she become the caretaker senator. Last week, right after Harris died, Dorothy told me that I have 'an obligation to carry on the Baker tradition' after all Harris and she had done for me. And the majority of the powers-that-be second her opinion."

"You must be feeling like Atlas with these burdens piling on your shoulders," Jennifer said delicately.

AGAINST ALL ODDS   53

"On top of everyone else's demands, I'm not even sure that I feel qualified to move up on the political totem pole," Ben continued with asperity. "I've been in the House for less than four years. I'm told that I'm a good, strong-minded, clear-thinking congressman who serves his district well. But it's a district of half a million constituents. A senator represents an entire state of five million people."

Ben blinked and shook his head as if overwhelmed by the enormity of the position. "And all this is happening at the same time that I'm beginning to question whether or not I want to dedicate my entire life to politics. They think I'm just getting started, while I'm considering getting out! My colleagues never realize that there might be some things I want to do for myself, instead of for them."

Jennifer's tone was strong and serene. "Don't talk so seriously, Ben. Not now. Everything is coming at you too quickly. Harris Baker was only laid to rest this week. There are many months till the election. The days will pass, and you'll make the right decisions when the time comes."

Ben stared at her, contemplating her words. Finally he gave a bright smile and stood up, pushing aside his empty plate. The sight of his very tall, powerful body stung Jennifer's imagination.

"Senator or congressman, if your district is in Missouri, you have the cartoons of Jennifer Aldrich to face." Then he added silkily, "Come over here. I want you close to me."

The command in his voice was unmistakable. Shakily Jennifer got up and went to him. She trembled with a mysterious apprehension as she leaned into the shield of his arms. Wordlessly they settled within the huge cushions of her long couch, not touching. Behind her she heard the stereo switch itself off. Silence.

Jennifer allowed herself to look fully into Ben's eyes. In the subdued lighting of the room they were the color of the deep sea. "You have such long eyelashes," she quietly told him.

In one easy motion his lips came down over hers. She burrowed comfortably into his arms, and kissing lightly, they reveled in the warmth and closeness of each other.

The actions of Ben's pliant mouth were triggering an exquisite yearning inside of Jennifer, and she tightened her slender arms about him, pushing her breasts hard against his upper chest. Her lips parted slightly, accepting the invasion of his caressing tongue, which darted in and out of her soft, full mouth.

Jennifer could feel her heart pounding as Ben's hands closed around the curve of her small waist, his thumbs barely pressing against her yielding stomach. The feather-light movements of his fingers on her jutting hipbones sent a shudder through her frame. She was rattled by the violence of her response to Ben's innocent touches, his delightful kisses.

Ben lifted his arms a little so he could comb his fingers through her wayward, deep brown tendrils.

"You're so special, Jennifer. You've got insight; you seem to know yourself so well. That's an attractive quality." The deepness of Ben's voice was pulling at Jennifer like the tang of a rare cologne. "But who would know that all those stalwart values are inside this dainty creature who looks like a young girl perpetually ready to go on an adventure? Oh, Sunshine, that little smile of yours could lift my spirits for weeks at a time."

He bent his head to the deep hollow at the base of her throat. He kissed, then nipped at the creamy shadow there. She sighed and slipped her hands under the collar of Ben's shirt, clinging to the firm muscles of his broad shoulders. He began an assault of kisses that rained over her forehead, her cheekbones, her earlobes.

She closed her eyes in joy, arching her neck. "What must you think of me, giving myself to you like this?" she murmured.

"Only that you must care for me the way I care for you," Ben replied huskily. "That you're feeling the same way I am right now."

Jennifer's arm circled around his neck like a curl of sea foam as he laid her down on the couch. His heavy weight pressed enticingly down over her, making her feel deliciously imprisoned. Her eyes glittered like the darkest topaz.

Hesitantly she fumbled at the buttons of his shirt. When it was off, she drew in her breath at the magnificence of his torso as it gleamed in the muted light. Ben did not have a muscleman's build, but he was well conditioned by exercise. His chest was covered by a soft tangle of springy, fragrant hair. Her fingers traveled over the wonder of his physique in a kind of celebration. She could feel his pantherlike muscles rippling under his skin.

His hands now held the soft weight of her round breasts. As he licked tantalizingly at the line of her jaw his fingertips carefully wandered over her sensitive nipples. They pressed, stiff with want, against the silk of her bra. Jennifer moaned, and Ben pressed his lips tightly over hers with an intimate, knowing movement, She could feel the telltale throbbing of his desire.

Their profiles were a whisper apart. "I've never felt this before," Jennifer said, her breath warm against Ben's.

"I've never wanted a woman the way I want you," he returned fiercely. He entangled his fingers in the tie of her wrap dress.

Breathless, she nodded in consent. Her fingertips strayed under the waistband of his jeans and her eyes closed expectantly as Ben tugged at the knot of her belt. He gently pushed open the dress, exposing the white softness of her body against the crimson jersey. In the shadowy room the filmy lace of her bra and underpants appeared transparent, revealing every curve and valley of her full body.

Her ardor was coming in waves of dizziness. Ben's knowing hand moved up her bare rib cage to the delicate clasp of her bra. She allowed him to unfasten it, no longer conscious of immodesty. Hardly touching her, he used one hand to span her nipples. "Ben," she gasped, absolutely carried away. She had surrendered completely to his loving mouth and fingers, yet in the midst of their mutual abandon they were smiling beatifically at one another, reveling in their closeness.

"You're ethereal," Ben told her softly. "You make me feel as though I can do things I wasn't able to do before." His mouth floated lightly above hers, as though he were daring himself not to kiss her. Then, he quickly seized her lips with immense passion.

In the heat of his kiss, his hand slipped down to lightly stroke the secret flesh of her inner thigh. Jennifer arched to meet his touch. She felt his thick hair against her bare shoulder and realized that she'd never experienced such lovely security and graceful unison. She was wild with her need for him, and her right hand twisted open the button of his jeans.

Then her hand froze there, as if she'd just cut her palm on a razor's edge. She pulled back in sudden alarm. What was happening? How had this happened?

"What's wrong?" Ben asked.

"I'm frightened."

"Why? There's nothing to be frightened of."

Bit by bit Jennifer extricated herself from Ben. She was shaking as she sat up. She didn't dare look at Ben. The direction they were headed would never allow her to forget him—her original, and instantly disregarded, plan for Representative Benjamin Trostel. "We shouldn't go any further than we're prepared to, Ben," she stammered, pulling her dress closed. "Thursday night we agreed to casually date. Remember? We're not free to do this, either of us!"

Apprehensively she glanced at him. His face was still full of tenderness. He reached for her carefully and caringly. She could smell his pleasing warm breath, and the electricity of his presence was almost overpowering. She only wanted to be crushed in his arms.

A self-protective reflex made her stand up abruptly and move into a chair opposite him. For a tense moment he glared at her uncomprehendingly, his brow knit with frustration. Both of them could tell that the strong spell was gradually dissolving. The sullenness melted from Ben's expression as the urgency ebbed in his veins, and he shrugged the flannel shirt back onto his bare shoulders. He moved to sit on the arm of her chair. Comfortingly, he massaged her neck with one hand.

"Perhaps you're right," he said slowly. He knew as

well as Jennifer that if they started anything, they would have to have everything. "There are some issues that we've been patently ignoring since you brought them up the other night."

"We're heading for something we can't possibly handle correctly." Jennifer's voice cracked slightly. Her brown eyes were wide and desperate. "We need to think about this more before anything else happens."

Now that she finally knew the man with whom things seemed so right, the man she could *love*, she was desperately afraid. True love would bring her hell as well as heaven. She couldn't frankly tell Ben this, not yet. So she spoke of the other problems that loomed between them.

"What do *you* think we should do?" she asked. She lifted her face toward him and saw that he was looking at her like a predatory animal longing to jump on his quarry. She quickly looked down at her hands, sitting in her lap like two limp little bodies.

Ben's soothing fingers stopped moving on her neck. "I don't want to pressure you or hurry you in any way, Jennifer. I could never make love to you, then rush off to the airport tomorrow morning."

"I know you couldn't."

They sat for a long while without speaking. They both understood what the other was thinking. They couldn't have each other in any casual sense, as if they were in an uncommitted relationship. Already they were too close, too understanding. There was too much fire between them.

Oblivious to his own magnificent appearance, Ben stood erect and stretched. Jennifer ran her fingers through her hair in a quick, nervous gesture as he began buttoning his shirt. Losing the sight of him was almost painful, and she turned away so that he wouldn't see her expression.

"It's not right for me to see you," she said. "I've successfully denied that to myself, but it's time to acknowledge the fact. My job is to be a watchdog against people in your profession, not cozy up to them! And right now, so much is happening to you...."

"You're right," Ben admitted. "I'm getting an overload, and you're part of it. The best part, but part nonetheless. Within the past few days I've grown dependent on you in many ways. It's never happened to me before like this." He sounded plaintive, bewildered.

"Do you like the feeling?" she asked cautiously.

Ben didn't answer directly. "How I wish you were coming with me to Washington tomorrow. I'd ask you to accompany me to the airport, but . . ." He put on his down vest, and Jennifer realized he was about to leave. She could feel herself collapsing inside, deflating like a dying balloon.

"We've both got a little thinking to do." Ben's tone was now cheerful, even diplomatic. "The situation is serious, but not hopeless. We need time apart to think about things, that's all. Why don't I call you when I get into Washington? And maybe we can see each other when I come back to town."

Jennifer nodded once, keeping her eyes dropped so that Ben couldn't see her distress. He bent at the waist to kiss the top of her head. As soon as she heard the front door close Jennifer sagged into the couch cushion.

She was profoundly, crushingly miserable, but it was her own fault. Seeing Ben, even talking to him as she had initially, was a risk from the start. Whenever she'd been interested in a man before, she had only been a child desiring a new toy. But Ben! He extended to her nothing less than a chance to fulfill life's promise.

At long last she had met a man who was her definite match, but he was forbidden to her by her profession. She may as well have been a nun, or Ben a priest. Because future Senator Trostel and cartoonist Jennifer Aldrich, syndicated in a hundred and seventy-five newspapers, could drop neither of their professions easily.

And what if she and Ben threw all caution to the winds and allowed themselves to get deeply, seriously involved? He lived in Washington. He *visited* St. Louis, where he had to be out constantly "pressing the flesh," trying to keep his voters and his party happy. Their relationship would be comprised solely of snatched moments. And if he ran for the Senate, the situation *would* be hopeless.

Jennifer turned on the television to an ancient black-and-white movie she couldn't identify. She huddled in front of the TV set, hollow and forlorn, and stared at it unseeingly until she fell into sleep.

Around noon on Sunday the phone rang. Jennifer picked it up with a dispirited "Hello?" She could hear the hum of long-distance wires and guess her parents were calling from their winter home in Arizona.

"What would you say if I told you that I miss you like crazy?" Ben demanded lightheartedly from Washington.

"That you're fully justified!" She was so happy to hear his voice. She added in a whisper, "I miss you so much."

A profound pause ensued. Then Ben said, "What would you say if . . . if I told you I love you?"

Jennifer's breath left her for a full second as her

consciousness was suspended in the air, quivering with joy. She responded evenly, "That you're impulsive. But that I feel the same way."

Ben's voice resonated sincerely over the miles, "I love you, Jennifer. I *need* you."

A euphoric look flooded over her already blushing face. She sank into a chair, weak with bliss. "And I love you, Ben."

Chapter Four

"Frank, I need some time off," Jennifer told her boss the first thing the following morning. "As soon as I can get it."

Quarters' bushy eyebrows went up. "This is kind of sudden."

"Not really. I've been thinking about vacation for a while now." Jennifer perched one hip on the edge of his desk. Here I am, she thought, wildly in love with a new source and trying to act nonchalant in front of the nose-for-news boss. "Think of it. I've been working on a treadmill without a break for a full year, churning out five cartoons a week come hell or high water. Just over the weekend I realized how badly I need a short break." How badly I need to be with Ben.

"I guess we could spare you for a week and run some cartoons from the syndicate in place of your work." Frank sighed, leaning back in his desk chair. A small but definite smile played over Jennifer's lips. "Finish out the week, then you can have the next week off." Conversationally he asked, "Where are you thinking of going?"

Jennifer reluctantly said, "Washington D.C. I've

never been there, and since I constantly draw the place and its denizens, I think it's about time I went."

"A working holiday, huh?" A shadow of puzzlement crossed over Frank's face. Jennifer knew that the perceptive editor would catch wind of her involvement with Representative Trostel sooner or later. She preferred later. He went on, "At this time of year, most people would prefer a vacation in the sun." Then he carelessly shrugged his shoulders. "I'll speak to the editor-in-chief about it, but I don't see any problem in getting you this short-notice break."

As Jennifer waited for Lynn Fantle-Johnson to meet her for dinner at the trendy little saloon near Busch Stadium she entertained herself by reliving in her imagination every minute she'd spent with Ben. She'd phoned him in Washington that day to tell him the time her flight would arrive on Friday. Though he was in his congressional office, he'd enthusiastically reminded her that he loved her.

"How can you smile like that when there's a blizzard outside?" Lynn demanded as she came up, shaking heavy flakes of snow from her coat. "On the way over I was sure that I'd lose my way in the storm and they'd find me frozen tomorrow morning, twelve feet from the door of this place."

A waiter appeared quickly to take their dinner order, then vanished. They were sitting at a marble-topped table with a wrought-iron base at the edge of a dark paneled room festooned with old tin and neon signs, antique statuettes and fake gas lighting fixtures. The room was populated with members of St. Louis's young professional crowd, and the gaiety of the surroundings only accented the buoyancy of Jennifer's mood.

"Lynn," she began carefully, "do you remember just

a couple of weeks ago when I was complaining to you about the absence of good, true, generous men in this town?"

"Sure. You said I'm married to the only one."

"I may have spoken too soon."

"What!" Lynn's round black eyes glowed with sudden interest. "You've met someone?"

"Not only have I met someone. We're in love. It's the first time it's really happened to me!"

Impatiently Lynn jumped, "Who is it?"

Jennifer spoke the next words like an actress pronouncing the most important line in a movie. "Ben Trostel. *The* Ben Trostel." An expression of shock—and apparent dismay—slowly crept over Lynn's face. Jennifer quickly added, "Don't tell anyone, least of all Frank Quarters."

As soon as Lynn's characteristic composure had returned she sat back in the cane chair and drawled, "Jenny, there are secrets . . . and then there are things that you don't tell *anyone*. This little item happens to fall into the latter category."

Their elaborate cheeseburgers arrived. Jennifer's grew cold as she related how she and the congressman had met, the events of the previous weekend and her upcoming trip to Washington. As she animatedly talked about Ben her usually impertinent features glowed unmistakably with passion and happiness. Lynn listened with a deadpan, slightly forbidding expression.

Finally she asked, "How do you know he wants you to come barnstorming out to Washington like this?"

"He asked me to come." Then she added, "It's only natural that he wants me to see how he lives and works. He loves me."

"How do you know he loves you?"

"He told me so. And I love him. That's all that matters."

Lynn shook her head with a long exhalation. "I don't know. It all sounds very abrupt to me."

"Sometimes the very best things happen very abruptly."

"I like Ben very much, Jenny. He's got independence, strength, intelligence, gentleness. He's also got a face and body a woman could weep for. You deserve him. But I don't know if it will work over the long haul."

Jennifer was offended. "Why? Because of the conflict-of-interest issue?"

"It *is* a dangerous situation," Lynn agreed. "Did I ever tell you about a friend of mine who was reporting for a paper in Oklahoma City? She was dating the president of the city council. That was unwise. Worse, she wrote glowing articles about him. *That* was suicide. When the editor learned about her innocent little affair, he fired her on the spot."

"Ben and I aren't in that kind of circumstance!" Jennifer scoffed. "I'd never let my personal feelings influence my cartoons. That'd be unethical."

"No. But she said she was in love with this guy, and that was 'all that mattered,' just as you're doing."

Jennifer shuddered with some vague premonition. "What happened to her after she was fired?"

"The affair with the council president fizzled out. She was left with no job, no husband, nothing. Today I think she's working on some tiny weekly in Alabama." Lynn waved her hand as if dismissing the subject. "However, you and Ben are in a particularly difficult position. Ben is at the start of a career that might take him anywhere in politics. And your job is to lampoon those in his profession. You can't deny that the professional gap between you two is bigger than the Grand Canyon. I can see you happy together now, but in the long run..."

"Our differences aren't personal, they're professional," Jennifer insisted.

"Whatever *that* means!" Lynn's eyes rolled heavenward, then back to her friend. Her tone became genuinely sympathetic as she said, "I don't mean to be a doomsayer, Jenny. I want things for you and Ben to work out. But as I said, this involvement, and the intensity of it, are pretty sudden. I don't want you to be hurt or disappointed if the whole relationship flares up and dies out like a meteor. As the cliché goes, that which burns brightest, burns fastest."

"Maybe so," Jennifer said heedlessly. The steadfastness of her feeling for Ben was impervious to any of Lynn's well-stated doubts... and by now, her own.

Jennifer was trembling with excitement when she boarded her plane early Friday afternoon. The 747 lifted her from the sorrowful gray Mississippi valley up through the clouds, where the sky was a clear, defined azure that reflected her mood. The idea of seeing Ben within a mere three hours was an overwhelmingly joyous one—and they hadn't even been separated a week!

She had treated herself to a first-class seat for this flight, and she sat enveloped in her new cashmere coat, thickly trimmed in fox fur. Though underneath she wore a heavy, white Icelandic sweater and gray wool gabardine trousers, she felt like Anna Karenina bound for a secret rendezvous with Count Vronsky.

She couldn't help but notice the portly man two seats ahead of her who was ordering around the flight attendants as though they were his personal valets. An hour after the flight departed she overheard him demand to forward an air-to-ground message "this very minute."

An ever-so-patient stewardess told the man that it couldn't be done. Jennifer heard him yelp, "But I'm a congressman. This is official government business."

The stewardess stalked away from him, past Jennifer, muttering, "A call to the wife is government business?"

That's when Jennifer finally recognized him as the U.S. representative from the congressional district adjoining Ben's. Like the attendants, she was amused and appalled by his autocratic behavior. The imperious congressman only confirmed her opinion of elected officials' inflated concept of their own importance.

The plane glided smoothly into Washington's Dulles Airport at four o'clock. At the signal to disembark Jennifer impatiently vaulted for the gate. Amid the usual jam of American tourists and exotically robed foreigners, she instantly spotted Ben. With his collar loose, tie undone, vest unbuttoned and hanging open and his opalescent blue eyes, he was heartbreakingly handsome.

"Congressman Trostel, I'd recognize you anywhere," she cried as they ran into each other's arms.

"I'm so glad you're here," he responded with a joyous laugh. They closed their eyes as they hugged one another fiercely, then kissed with a hunger that only separation could create. They drew back to look at each other; their fingertips barely touching the other's face in wonder.

"I've got something for you," Jennifer purred coyly, reaching into her butter-soft leather satchel. She took out the original of the "Excalibur" cartoon, protected by thin cardboard.

"Thank you," Ben exclaimed in pleasure as his eyes once again studied the drawing. "And to think you made this special trip just to hand-deliver it."

"You're worth it," Jennifer teased in return, placing the portfolio back in her bag.

Ben was suddenly serious as he looped his arms tighter around her and looked down into her wide, melting eyes. "I can't believe you're here," he said in a low voice. "And I can't believe everything that's happened between us. But I'm so certain about it, honey."

Jennifer stood gazing at him, speechless. All she could think of was that she loved him, and wanted to give herself to him. Now.

"Let's go get my luggage."

A porter lifted Jennifer's garment bag and suitcase into a taxi while the young couple eased themselves into the rear seat. They sat a few inches apart, their fingers interwoven in contentment, as the taxi entered the rush-hour squall. In no time at all they were over a bridge and passing Jefferson Memorial, traveling to Rock Creek Parkway.

Jennifer instantly identified the Mall, lined by the familiar historic structures of the Lincoln Memorial, the Capitol building and the Smithsonian museums. Each colossal, white marble edifice blazed in a fluorescent pink provided by the last rays of the winter sun. A recent rain had frozen over the existing layer of snow with a spun-sugarlike glaze that made the Mall resemble a child's birthday cake.

How much longer will this ride last, Jennifer wondered edgily as she watched traffic surge through the capital's many arteries, its harsh noises muted by slush and banks of snow. She vibrated with a curious blend of shy apprehension and savage desire. In the light of dusk, Ben's fascinating eyes and golden-toned face looked like that of an icon. She admired the shadows cast by his long cheekbones. As she breathed in the faint scent of his cologne she decided that Ben Trostel was nothing less than a walking, talking invitation. The electric current that coursed between them was made eloquently apparent by their very silence.

Finally the cab let them off at the lobby of the Watergate Hotel, a massive C-shaped building that many representatives used as their Washington address. The couple had the elevator to themselves, and Ben took a moment to give Jennifer a scintillating kiss. He slid his hands under her unbuttoned cashmere coat and held her around her rib cage, just under her breasts. Her response was instantaneous and urgent. They both knew what was going to happen between them tonight.

"This is my first visit to Washington," Jennifer said liltingly as they stepped off the elevator, "and I'm here with my congressman! Funny, though, the Capitol and current events hold no interest for me right now."

"Isn't that disgusting?" Ben clucked. In a mellifluous voice he continued, "I should be relating to you all the fascinating details of my last week on the hill, Sunshine. But you're such a breathtaking gust of fresh air that you've made me apathetic about the stuffy, dull proceedings of my legislative life."

He opened the door to his apartment. The layout was similar to that of his St. Louis studio, except that there was a door that obviously led to a bedroom.

Again his living room was dominated by a wall-sized window. This one revealed the dark Potomac River, its turbid and partially frozen water shining like a black opal.

Ben set down Jennifer's bags and kissed her dimpled cheek before withdrawing a bottle of Bollinger R.D. Tradition from an ice bucket. "This is for you—to celebrate your first trip to the cradle of democracy."

"You're a sweetheart! How thoughtful!" Jennifer's slight overenthusiasm revealed her nervousness. Ben looked at her pointedly before he poured the clear liquid into two fluted champagne goblets.

"I just found out why tulip champagne glasses are shaped like this," he said, handing one to her. "The small mouth of the glass concentrates the bouquet, since less of the champagne is exposed to the air. A wide, shallow wineglass will dissipate the full flavor of a good champagne."

"Interesting," Jennifer replied distractedly. His scrupulous, almost fussy attention to the ritual would have struck her as cute if she had not had her mind so intently on other things. She lifted her goblet and clinked it lightly against Ben's. "To . . ."

". . . us," he obliged. They silently tasted the refreshing liquid, then he said, "Why don't we step over to the window? You can see the Arlington memorials across the river, all lit up."

They had brought a tension to the high-ceilinged room, contradicting the overall sense of ease created by the warm colors of the graceful furniture and the fine prints on the book-lined walls. Unlike his sterile Missouri residence, this place of Ben's was thoroughly lived-in. It looked like a comforting retreat for a man who enjoyed his hours alone.

Jennifer pointed at a document-strewn desktop and inquired, "Is that all work? All 'official government business'?"

"Yes." Ben exhaled, running a hand through his thick, already-rumpled hair. Jennifer wanted to kiss his hairline where the light brown silkiness started to grow. "I've got a workload that would break a Clydesdale's back. I'll thoroughly ignore it for the next week, naturally."

They stood apart at the window, gazing at the headlights of the rush-hour traffic across the river, sipping pleasurably at the chilled, effervescent champagne. After a beat, Ben spoke slowly and longingly. "I could make reservations. We could go and eat." There was a pause. "Or we could stay here."

The chemistry between them was working in full force. Jennifer regarded him over the rim of her goblet. Her eyes were large and innocent, like a child's. She could name none of the feelings running through her. She set the glass down on an end table and guilelessly said, "I've thought about you endlessly."

"I've thought about you. The way you walk, the color of your eyes. Your jasmine scent." Ben's words were sharp and direct, a statement instead of a compliment. Jennifer's gaze on his finely shaped, sensual features turned into a burning stare. He too set down his glass.

Simultaneously they yielded to a mutual, silent command and gathered their arms around each other. Their kiss was immediately wild and turbulent, their hands gliding over each other's backs. The slight roughness of Ben's tongue sent shivers of sensation through Jennifer, from the soles of her feet to the roots of her hair.

After an indefinite time she drew back so they could look at one another. They were both panting slightly as their hearts beat excitedly. If they could both stop at this moment, suspend time, they could escape, have more time to think about the journey they were about to embark on.

Ben took both of Jennifer's hands in his. The room was illuminated only by the outside floodlights reflecting through the huge window, but his eyes glittered brightly. "What's wrong?" he inquired with softness. "Are you afraid of something?"

"I'm not afraid, I'm anticipating," Jennifer stammered. "I'm a little uncertain of my need right now. Everything is happening so fast. I'm not an impulsive person; but you've turned me into one."

"You and I will make love with love," Ben insisted, his voice hardly audible. "We've been intended for this from the day we met. You know it's going to all turn out."

Jennifer's lips barely moved. "Of course."

His lips grazed her temple along the hairline. With a sigh Jennifer relaxed and looked up at his face. As she did so Ben pressed his lips on hers. She again savored the feeling of his tongue sweeping languorously inside her mouth and the heat of his palms around her small waist.

This is right, she thought light-headedly, slipping her hands up under his rear shirttail. This *is* the culmination of something that has been determined for us since we've known each other. I *want* to lose myself in him, I want to drown in him.

Her body started to throb with a desire she'd never thought existed. She pulled at Ben's forearms and they simultaneously eased themselves into a sitting position on the carpet without interrupting their embrace. They were kissing, merely kissing, but Jennifer found herself so hot and uncomfortable in the Icelandic sweater that she impetuously yanked it off over her head and let it fall on the floor. Ben instantly drew off the camisole underneath.

He sat there for a long moment, staring unabashedly at her well-rounded breasts. They stood out fine and clear within the shadows of the room, the nipples barely darker than the surrounding flesh. "You're so lovely," he murmured then. His hands reached to cover the soft, yielding skin as though they were holding something precious, and he leaned to kiss at the long line of her throat. Jennifer fell against the carpet, floating, dissolving and reemerging. She threw her head back as her body abandoned itself to him. "You are so insinuating," she muttered huskily. "Absolutely irresistible."

"Oh, I do love you," Ben responded against her neck, where a pulse beat.

Jennifer looked down as his hands moved from her breasts around to the indented vertical line in the midst of her smooth back, and then further, further down. Her trousers began to slip away, and Ben's hands curved into the heart of her throbbing desire. She sucked in her breath, amazed that his overwhelmingly strong hands could become so sweetly soft when placed in the right places.

Their clothes came away till the two of them lay in splendid, warm nudity. Jennifer tentatively stroked different parts of Ben's torso and arms, exploring and discovering. "I can't believe the different textures of your body," she said with plaintive wonder. "Your skin is so smooth here"—she glided her palms over his biceps—"so rough on your chin."

Her small hands finally reached for his magnificent hardness, which was distinct among the shadows of his thighs and private hair. As she lingered there he brought his mouth down to her breasts. His lips tugged exquisitely at the light pink rosettes till they strained to erect points of concentrated, thrilled response and were transformed to a deep rose shade.

All of Jennifer's senses—touch, scent, sight, hearing—were overflowing. She was aware of only herself and Ben within their private, humming space. At last Ben gripped her around the waist and thrust himself inside her. She stiffened, then relaxed and entwined her strong, limber legs around his in a graceful arabesque. His flesh was firmly enclosed in hers.

"I've . . . I've never felt anything like this before," Ben gasped. His warm, moist breath mingled with Jennifer's as they strained together. "You are so incredible, honey. You make me want to love you all the time."

They rocked together voluptuously in a perfectly matched rhythm. They were enveloped by a vast silence. Even their breathing was steady and quiet as their bodies were gliding and swooping and moving as one.

All of Jennifer's physical senses were concentrated excruciatingly in her lower region as she gazed absorbedly into Ben's darkly impassioned face. She pressed against him and abruptly felt a sharp tingle deep within her belly, a sensation of amazing ecstasy. She uttered one choked cry as the thrill passed like lightning to the ends of her toes. At the same time her eyelids fluttered closed. His hands convulsively gripped her shoulders, and she and Ben trembled in a mutual climax like two saplings shaken by the strongest gale. Behind her eyelids Jennifer saw tiny colored lights exploding, fireworks that accompanied the feelings that raged through their bodies.

A moment later they fell apart, gleaming with perspiration, gasping from the physical passion that had overcome them. She felt heavy and satiated with their rich lovemaking. The descent back to reality was gradual and reluctant.

Eventually Jennifer rose on one elbow to reach for a cord-mounted lamp switch. The sudden light revealed the sparkle dancing in Ben's eyes and the white radiance of his smile. He enfolded her peacefully in his arms and kissed her again. She enjoyed the sensation of her softened nipples being tickled by the hair on his chest.

"Would it be redundant, after what we've just created here, for me to say I love you?" Ben asked in a deep, infinitely feeling voice.

"I'll never stop needing to have you tell me that," Jennifer responded ardently. She kissed the gold skin at the nape of his neck.

"Good. Then I will say it as often as I like," Ben said decisively, pulling Jennifer tighter to him. "And when I say love, I mean love."

Chapter Five

Heavy snow fell from the silver-gray morning sky, making the bedroom look unusually light for that time of day. Half covered by a satiny duvet quilt, Jennifer held her slight, lithe body over Ben's long, hard one. Her fingers languorously combed his hair, which she surmised was several weeks overdue for a cut.

"I've never been this relaxed in my life," Ben was saying slowly in a rather drowsy voice. His strong brown arms were wrapped around Jennifer's back and his face looked up at hers. "I never dreamed that this could happen to me."

Me neither, Jennifer thought. "Why not?" she asked gravely.

"I'm thirty-one, Sunshine. All my friends have been married for years. While I've kept plodding on—working, meeting people, studying issues and laws, campaigning—they've been starting families, living happily. I feel like everything I do, I've done before.

"I'm the veteran of too many dates and one two many fleeting relationships. And every woman I met only confirmed and repeated the hopelessness of ever finding someone I would treasure. I was beginning to believe that falling in love was a sign of weakness."

Ben was expressing the same disappointments that had always echoed through Jennifer's life. She could never have found the words, though, as he was doing so unerringly. She listened without interrupting.

"I know we've tumbled headlong into this, Jennifer. But within a few hours of meeting you, I recognized that you were someone who would *depend* on me without being *dependent*. You listen to me, you want to know what I think. But ultimately you make your own decision. Jennifer Aldrich, you are almost too good to be true."

Ben drew her lips down to his, and Jennifer absorbed into her senses the warm scent of his skin, a sweet contrast to the lovely patterns of snow drifting past the window. The picturesqueness of the surroundings only served to amplify the fairy-tale unreality of the love she and Ben had discovered together.

Representative Benjamin Trostel was one of the least effective members of the United States Congress as the following week flew by, time out of mind. For the first time in his career he skipped committee meetings, repeatedly missed the roll call on the House floor, ignored phone messages. When he did show up on the floor for one important vote, he craned his head around to the visitors' gallery so often to look at Jennifer he finally gave up and came upstairs to sit with her until it was time for his "yea."

The marble and brocade hallways of the Capitol, the commotion of meeting Ben's colleagues and the names of famous restaurants and historical places intertwined in Jennifer's thoughts with the euphoric bliss of knowing Ben. Every day was more wonderful than the last. Each evening they made love, and talked and laughed far into the night.

Just walking with Ben was an experience. He pointed out the landmarks and explained them in such a way that he transformed the capital into a giant playground that Jennifer rushed through happily. He could point out a passerby and with a simple observation like "There's last year's second runner-up in the Groucho Marx Lookalike Contest," have her nearly rolling on the ground in convulsed laughter.

"Sometimes I feel like such an openmouthed simpleton," she protested to him while strolling down a winter-crisp Pennsylvania Avenue. "I just hang on your arm begging for more stories, making you do all the work."

"Listen, you," Ben chastised, "watching you enjoy this old town is providing me with so much enjoyment ... in fact, I'm probably having twice as much fun as you are."

"Impossible. That would mean I'm having half as much fun as you," Jennifer squealed, making Ben laugh happily as they continued their arm-in-arm walk past the White House.

The pure tenderness of the couple's feelings for one another was always part of their bursts of passion. Each kiss, each caress they shared, was complete in itself, till every love act meant much more than simple physical gratification.

Jennifer was amazed that Ben Trostel, with his lanky cowboy looks, could be so voracious, masterful and passionate. His lovemaking not only took her to heights of sensual ecstasy she'd never thought possible, but he made her feel so *good* about herself. This eminently desirable man was willing to spend hours hugging her, stroking her, doing his best to please her while the rest of the world faded from their shared existence.

As Jennifer washed her hair Wednesday night she reflected how she often felt she had developed a protective armor as she forged her way through the harsh, competitive working world. Now, watching her face in the bathroom mirror as she massaged the scented shampoo through her ringlets, she could see for herself how her face was marvelously alive. Her enormous eyes looked like twin pools of chocolate satin reflecting candlelight, where before she'd always thought they looked very ordinary. Ben had magically dissolved her invisible toughness, making her feel uniquely soft and delicate, as airy as an iridescent soap bubble.

Lost in thought, she dazedly watched the soapsuds gurgle down the bathroom sink as she rinsed them from her head. She fantasized about the lovely emotion running between her and Ben. Theirs was a wonderful whirlwind involvement, underlined by permanent implications she couldn't allow herself to think about. She'd become too giddily overexcited if she did.

As she towel-dried her hair the phone rang once in the other room. She peeked out of the bathroom and saw Ben holding the receiver. He was wearing a kelly-green lamb's-wool sweater with old jeans that fit him so snugly she was jealous of every woman who had ever looked at him. His expression was concerned and attentive as he listened to the caller.

Jennifer turned back and finger-combed her hair. After a while she wrapped herself in Ben's huge terrycloth bathrobe and joined him in the living room. He stood in the center, hands jammed deep into his pockets, staring blankly at the oriental rug under his feet.

"Ben?"

As he looked up tension passed over his face as quickly and faintly as the shadow of a bird. Then he smiled comfortably. Gathering Jennifer's warm, clean body into his arms, he kissed the top of her damp head, then eased her down beside him on his long couch. "That was Dorothy Baker, calling from Jefferson City," he said. Jennifer felt something inside her tighten up. "Tomorrow she'll publicly announce that she's accepting the governor's appointment to her husband's senate seat, but only as a caretaker. She's going to stress that she's not running for it this fall."

"She must be terribly busy. Why couldn't one of her aides have phoned you instead?"

"She called personally to announce sort of a command performance, I guess. Dorothy wants me to attend her at her swearing-in here next Monday. She seemed to think she'd be doing me a great favor."

"I don't quite understand."

"My presence at her side during her induction as Missouri's senator is virtually Mrs. Baker's endorsement for my bid for the upcoming Senate race."

Why didn't Ben sound elated at this endorsement instead of the littlest bit sour? Any other Missouri politician would have considered a blessing from Harris Baker's widow to be heaven sent. Jennifer fingered the wisps of light hair that curled over the V-neck of his sweater, then looked up at his eyes, which at the moment resembled dull sapphire chips. "Don't you want Mrs. Baker to help you?"

"Well, for one thing, I haven't even announced for the doggone race."

"For that matter, neither has anyone else." Jennifer paused. "Why aren't you happy about her endorsement? I know you've talked about getting out of politics eventually, but . . ."

After a moment he said, "I've never told this to anyone, baby. I have plenty of solid faith in my own ability, but ever since my first run for Congress I've often felt like I've been riding on Harris Baker's coattails. I have the feeling that for the rest of my political life, no matter how much I accomplish, I'll always be known as Harris's protegé. The news stories will always read, 'Young Trostel got his start with a generous helping hand from Senator Baker.'"

"I assume you don't want his family to maintain a 'coattail' tradition, then," Jennifer said. She knew Ben was quite troubled. "Did Baker actually help you that much?"

Ben's eyes filled with a memory. "Just five years ago I was having a great time being Harris's man in St. Louis, another anonymous lawyer who sold a magazine article every once in a while. Then the congressional seat in the St. Louis district opened up, and Harris and his cronies urged me to run for it."

"You were reluctant about the idea?"

"At first, yes. I had planned on practicing law and free-lancing until I could support myself entirely by writing. But I've always wanted to help people somehow, and I knew Harris's offer was a real opportunity."

"Writing *is* a way of helping people. The pen is mightier than the sword, supposedly."

"I've always felt that. But you also have to admit that you can help people a lot more effectively, or directly, as a politician. The high congressman's salary, the prestige and the benefits of the position were like a carrot on a stick. I knew I could retire after several terms, if I liked. The race looked relatively easy, and Harris's influence was a solid asset. So I ran."

Ben sighed and tilted his fine head so it rested on her shoulder. She could feel his warmth through their layers of clothes. His eyes were on the window as he continued. "I began knocking on every door in the district. Though my opponent didn't campaign as hard, we were near even in the polls. Then a month before the election, the media discovered that the guy was having a torrid affair with his campaign manager."

"Was he married?"

"Married! His own wife broke the story to the papers—his campaign manager was *her* brother's wife! Isn't that wild? My passage into Congress was about as 'greased' as it could be. So to this day I have to wonder, would I have won that first race without the scandal? Did I win the seat on my own merits, on the issues?"

"Ben, darling, you forget about your somewhat winning personality," Jennifer protested lovingly. "Your smiling, handsome face showing up at voters' doors might have bewitched some folks, you know."

Ben grunted disparagingly. "I've never fully understood the ramifications of that 'golden boy' tag, either. Even though I've worked like a dog since I've been on the Hill—if I had a family I'd never see it!—I often feel as though everything I've attained has been presented to me on a silver platter. Sometimes I even feel a little guilty, or unworthy of my position."

"How can you say that?" Jennifer chastised. She was shocked by his statement. Here was a man who was debating whether he should run for the Senate, with his party encouraging him to do so, and yet he didn't feel good about being a representative.

"Look at your situation, Jennifer, in contrast to mine. You've always won your cartooning jobs and your reputation on your own talent. You've never needed the services of a sponsor."

"That's not true," she rejoined. "I never had to 'claw my way to the top' exactly. I was always lucky enough to submit my portfolio to people who were willing to give me a break. Oh, Ben, can't you see that you have earned your position, that you've earned all the great respect you're given both here and in Missouri, all by yourself! You've made it on your own!" She shook her head from side to side. "Most politicians are so vain. They don't have doubts like this. Do you think you have enough drive to go out and win that Senate seat, honey? Enough focused will and want?"

Again Ben did not answer her question directly. He continued testily, "The whole possibility of running for the Senate seat only underscores, in my mind, the dissatisfactions I've known in the House—gripes that have been building over the past four years." He seemed to be talking as much to himself as to Jennifer as he told her about the way his work could easily consume eighty to a hundred hours of his time every week; about the lack of job security and the high cost of every campaign; about the abuse he received from constituents who were eager to blame him for everything but the weather; about how he had to be accountable at all times to his voters; about the constant phone calls and requests from lobbyists, constituents and special-interest groups. Jennifer had witnessed some of these problems for herself within the past several days.

"It sounds as though the rewards of elected office don't always compensate for the stress they involve," she observed.

Ben looked blindly out the window a moment, thinking. He looked at her again, and his face became more animated as he said, "Still Jennifer, I *do* find public service downright addictive, because I'm able to do good for people in tangible ways. Sometimes with a new law, sometimes with a simple phone call. What you do *matters*. If I did get the Baker Senate seat, I could do even more."

He stood up and made an abrupt gesture in the direction of Arlington. "And when you boil it all down— after the mediocre politicians, after all the pettiness and bureaucracy of government—what you have left is history. That's what everything in this town stands for."

He was clearly pushing all doubts out of his mind. As he leaned down to pull Jennifer to him his face was vivid with a too-sudden cheerfulness. "Time to dress, my beautiful girl. We've got reservations for eight at Dominique's."

Much later, Jennifer raised herself on one elbow to watch Ben sleep beside her. He was turned toward her, his head cradled by fluffy down pillows. In the muted light radiating from the snow-heavy clouds outside, she studied the perfection of his features, his long eyelashes, the graceful musculature of his arms and torso. Well, he should sleep she thought. He had risen an hour before her that morning to jog the entirety of the Mall, then worked out at a gym.

AGAINST ALL ODDS 85

She brushed her lips against his. Since Dorothy Baker's phone call, she'd been invaded by a grim uneasiness. Ben was at a crucial turning point in his personal and professional life. And Jennifer, whom he felt was so close to, was incapable of advising him on his decision. To say she was unobjective and uninformed was an understatement.

She had not yet made peace with herself over the unresolved, perhaps unresolvable, issues that dangled over them like a sword of Damocles. There was the conflict of professional interests, of course. She could still hear Lynn's panicky warnings about that, when she allowed herself to. Then there was the fact that dealing with politicians left her cool, if not downright cold. In truth, Jennifer did not want to share Ben's political life completely. Did that mean her love for him was shallow?

No! Jennifer thought fiercely. His feeling for politics isn't of vital essence to him; it's like a coat he can put on or take off, she told herself. He'll probably take off this figurative coat for good within a couple of years.

And in that, in many ways she enjoyed Ben's status as a representative. *He* certainly didn't leave her cold. But what if his next campaign was for the Senate? That was the thorny question that wouldn't leave the back of her mind. She didn't want him to become Senator Trostel. Instinctively she knew Ben wouldn't be happy in the more demanding and prominent government position.

"Oh, I hope you don't run!" she whispered intently at Ben's faintly breathing form.

He opened his eyes, which shone like lasers in the dark. "What did you say?" he asked alertly.

Slightly flustered, Jennifer didn't reply, but buried her face in his lustrous, fragrant hair. One of his hands moved down to stroke her belly. She leaned into his arms, pressing herself against him, and as they began to move together her thoughts of a few moments before dispersed like so many rain clouds. She became aware only of the moment. And Ben. His mouth, his touch—above everything, Ben.

Chapter Six

As Jennifer entered Frank Quarters' office Monday morning she looked like a schoolgirl being summoned to the principal's office. The door shut behind her with an ominous click.

"Just a second," Quarters muttered as he scribbled in the margins of a typewritten article. Jennifer folded herself somewhat jerkily into the chair that faced his plain oak desk. She studied the adjoining beige wall, scattered with framed journalism awards and certificates. They'd been hung, then forgotten; each glass had collected years of dust.

Finally, Frank looked up while slapping the story onto a pile of papers on his desk. "What'd you want to see me about, Jenny?" he asked jovially.

"Frank, do you remember when we were talking about Ben Trostel, and the fact that I'd have to draw a lot of cartoons about him?" Jennifer began cautiously. Frank nodded once, his eyes closing and opening portentously. "Well, we've got a problem."

"Which is?"

"I met Trostel several weeks ago. We've started a relationship."

"A relationship?"

"An involvement, an affair."

"An affair . . ." Quarters already knew the full implications of her hesitant phrases, but he was going to force her to state it aloud.

"It's serious, Frank. Maybe 'serious' is an understatement."

"And I suppose this week in Washington . . ." Frank's tone reeked of disdain.

"We had to confirm everything, after knowing each other for such a short time." Oh, how could someone be simultaneously so happy and so full of trepidations as she was now? "Things might not have worked out. But everything *is* perfect, and I wanted you to be the first to know, before anyone else found out."

"Thanks for the favor." Frank's sarcastic growl was savagely disgusted. He took a cigar out of his pocket. "You're not doing yourself any favors, y'know. This innocent little romance of yours is going to be a black mark on your career forever."

"Not necessarily," Jennifer replied somewhat weakly.

"No, Jenny," he snapped scornfully, "a political cartoonist wields awesome power. You can sway public opinion like few others. And you've compromised your integrity by playing footsie with a subject of your work, a source! I've seldom heard a case of such extreme conflict of interest."

His raisin eyes fastened on her and he continued mercilessly. "Not only are you involved with Trostel, but by implication you're involved with his political party, with the Baker legacy—a network of politicos too numerous to think of! Each of your cartoons is the St. Louis *Herald*'s opinion as well as your personal opinion. This cozy fellowship with Trostel and his ilk automatically taints this newspaper's positions." A little grunt of repugnance issued from his throat. "Cartoonists traditionally avoid even associating with politicians after they've met them. They fear that friendship will take the sharpness out of their serpent's tooth."

Jennifer felt he was exaggerating the severity of her offense. Slightly emboldened, she countered, "I didn't set out to make friends with Ben. It just happened."

"That old black magic, eh?"

Jennifer ignored the comment. "My portrayal of Ben and his party will be as nasty as ever, when necessary." She leaned forward and said intently, "His politics, and his party line, aren't for me to follow. And neither are the other party's! I have no doubt that I'll remain absolutely objective in my work. In my head everything is still equal, still balanced."

"If everything isn't equal in your heart, eh? Well no matter what you may think, in your subconscious some things are going to be a lot more equal than others. Sorry, but you have to make a choice. Dump Trostel . . . or dump your job."

Jennifer's face paled under her dark mop of curls. Her brown eyes rounded with despair, but she managed to control her voice. "It's not that easy. Not that clear-cut."

Frank's inflection was much less gruff. "Your career is going to sustain you the rest of your life. Do you honestly think *he* is going to last that long?"

In a small voice Jennifer ventured, "Marriage is a possibility, I suppose."

Frank looked at her in silence, and she could see the wrath in him begin to uncoil. He lit his cigar, then puffed on it slowly. "All right. A compromise. Until the election, no cartoons that involve Trostel, Dorothy Baker or the Senate race." He shook his head ruefully. "It's a bad solution. The whole Baker-Trostel issue is of primary news importance, and now our cartoonist won't be able to cover it. If you were anyone else, Jenny, if you had less talent . . ." *You would have been fired.* The unspoken sentence hung over her like a noose.

Paternal concern entered his voice as he said, "Y'know, *I* personally trust your judgment. I honestly can believe that your hand-holding with Trostel isn't going to shade the viewpoints in your work. But what would our readers think about this paper's policies when they find out that our cartoonist is dating this state's next senator?"

"That won't happen!" Jennifer's face showed her horror of the limelight. Frank's derisive laughter told her that once again she was attempting to deny the inevitable. As "Glamour Boy" Trostel's girl friend, she would probably be a minor celebrity.

Cagily, Frank pressed on. "So. Is Trostel going to run for the Senate?"

"I don't know," she half lied, knowing that Ben was leaning against the race for higher office at this point. It was possible that he might not even run for his House seat again, but she'd never let out that secret. "And if I did, I couldn't give the *Herald* that scoop anyway. Conflict of interest, you understand."

"If you didn't occupy such a unique slot in the journalism hierarchy, you'd be terminated for sure." Frank spoke lightly, but he was stating a fact. He grudgingly added, "Be happy, kid." He stood up. "I like Trostel a lot. He's okay for a horse thief."

"Glad you agree," Jennifer said dryly, also rising.

Frank studied the end of his cigar. A thought made him chuckle, and he returned to an earlier part of the conversation. "Marriage? No, you could never be a mealy mouthed little politician's wife. You'd choke to death biting on your own tongue!"

Jennifer returned to her office, plopped into her chair and petulantly smoothed her box-pleated skirt. Outside the skyline resembled a hulking robotic monster.

She should have been feeling as relieved and cleansed as a sinner who'd just repented, yet she was dissatisfied and surly inside. She and Frank had resolved the conflict of interest problem in only a halfhearted way. Her job was to follow all issues impartially. She was doing the *Herald* and its readers a grave disservice by eliminating the upcoming Senate race and related issues from her editorial space.

Oh, the hell with it! She sulked, running her hands through her ringlets. It was high time she made some sacrifices for her personal life.

But what about that last little crack of Frank's, about being a "mealymouthed politician's wife"? Why did that strike such an irritating chord in her?

"Anyone could tell *you're* in love," Lynn told her at the end of February. She waved toward the boxes stacked on a file drawer in Jennifer's office. "Every other lunch hour you go out and buy these extravagant . . . things!"

"I can't help it," Jennifer responded with a grin. "It's hard to explain, but I feel like injecting a little graciousness into my life."

"That's what love is all about, girl. It makes you come fully alive."

Since Jennifer had returned from Washington, she'd been purchasing personal items that appealed to the feminine, sensuous aspects in her makeup that had been half buried for so long. She now owned a wardrobe of creamy, pastel lingerie, lace-edged linen and a cosmetic-counterful of subtle perfumes, lotions and powders.

Ben had awakened her basic feminine identity. He had returned to her the childlike ability to find great pleasure in ordinary things. And he had shown her her own ability to gain grandly exquisite pleasure from extra-special things. He kept her going with long, intimate nightly phone calls. And at that very moment, she was admiring the way the sunlight pushed through the translucent petals on the tulips he had sent her the day before.

"Listen, you're going to have to forgive me for all those doubts I expressed about Ben," Lynn said, standing before her drawing-board desk.

"No, they were understandable," Jennifer demurred. "He'll be in town this weekend. How about you and David stepping out for dinner with us?"

"Sounds good. I don't remember the last time I had dinner with a congressman."

"I do. The Missouri Association of Independent Bankers Convention in Jefferson City last week. You told me you had four of them to your table."

"There are congresspeople—and then there's Old Blue Eyes Ben Trostel!" Lynn smiled and exited with her usual distinctive gracefulness.

A few minutes later the ring of the phone shattered the room's quietness. Jennifer was delighted to hear

Ben's voice on the other end. He wanted to know if she could pick him up at the airport in a few hours.

"Oh, Ben! Of course I can."

"I booked the earliest plane I could," his voice crackled longingly from Washington. "I can't wait to hold you again. Besides," he added, "I have something important to tell you."

After work Jennifer half jogged to the gourmet shop, where she bought cold meats, cheeses, stone-ground bread and a variety of the freshest fruits. At the last moment she chose several bouquets of lilacs and freesia and had them wrapped securely against the cold. She hurried back to her condominium and changed into a jacquard silk blouse with a jabot and puffed shoulders, and a maroon jersey skirt. Then she hurried to the airport.

Jennifer felt an opulent joy creep over her as soon as she saw Ben walking through the gate. It started in her stomach, moved to her back and up her shoulders to her neck. Then he was with her, possessively circling his arms around her slender back. They kissed like two people in a fairy tale who had been separated for years but always bound together by a promise and the matching halves of a broken amulet they had treasured. It had been twelve days since they'd seen each other.

"Coming back is the best part of leaving you, Jennifer," Ben declared, clutching her tightly. He wore corduroy jeans and a soft, wool sweater under a worn leather coat. As she laid her fingers over his broad chest she simultaneously reveled in the feel of his sweater, the oxford shirt beneath it and the crisp chest hair and the warm skin under it all.

"It's strange I didn't realize just how much I missed

you till just now. It hurts," she cried, vibrating with both pleasure and yearning.

"I know exactly what you mean," he murmured quietly into her hair. He carried only one bag, so they went directly to her silver Ford compact in the parking lot.

"Look," Ben said impishly, pointing at the cold tarmac under their feet. "See how the floodlights throw our shadows together on the ground? There's a saying that when two people walk side by side and their shadows join like that, they'll be together for the rest of their lives."

His words had the ring of a prophecy. Jennifer gave him a bright, trembling smile. He stopped in his tracks to kiss her deeply and demandingly.

As they talked excitedly during the ride back to her apartment, Jennifer was again struck by Ben's interest in *her,* in what mattered to her. There was so much about her life that she'd never told anybody, that nobody had ever seemed interested in. . . . But he made her want to share it all with him.

They removed their shoes at the door of her condominium. They crossed the rugs silently, enjoying the lovely hush in the large space.

"Alone with you, finally," Ben said in a fierce whisper. He took her head between his two large hands and kissed her forehead. Jennifer gazed at his lips, shaking with the compulsion to kiss them, to caress his face with her fingertips. Her senses were hypercharged. Collecting herself, she turned away on stocking feet and indicated the lush spread she had laid out on the table.

"This is for you," she announced proudly.

"For me?" Ben regarded the platters before him.

"Whatever happened to your toast flambé?" She could tell his mind was more on her than it was on her canapés, but he was going to be graceful enough to appreciate the effort she'd gone to. "I'll take one of each," he said, picking up a strawberry, one blue ribier grape and a ripe peach. He bit into the peach, then gave it to Jennifer. Watching him, aflame with his closeness, her small teeth pierced lightly at the same spot he had bitten from.

Ben's vision seemed blurred with sensuality as he looked at her, and his cool blue eyes were half lidded as he said, "I don't want any more food now, Jennifer." He took the peach from her as if she were a child and set it back on the plate with the other fruit.

His mouth sought out her upturned lips. They kissed slowly, the faint peach taste still on their lips, savoring, sharing, giving to one another. Jennifer could feel the simple physical systems that held her body upright quickly turn to liquid.

Ben drew her to his sturdy chest, and she breathed in his clean, intoxicating smell. "This is incredible," he exclaimed softly. "I'm feeling the same excitement and nervousness that I did the very first time."

She looked up, and her brown eyes glistened like dark jewels of desire. "I love you, Benjamin," she uttered as the feeling swelled through her like a melody.

"My little love. You look beautiful tonight," he answered. She arched her back and pressed her length against his tall, lean body, easily feeling his hardness at her lower belly. To the depths of her, she craved his masculine power. Her fingers tightened instinctively around his upper arms, her signal to him that she was impatient, that she needed his strength now. He scooped her slender body up in his arms. She lay securely, spellbound, her head draped on his wide shoulder. He moved to the bedroom, carrying her like a precious bundle.

The room was lit by a single white globe that rewarmed their haven of sensual charm, an atmosphere quite different from her sleek living room. The room was dominated by billowy curtains, satin pillows threaded with ribbon, bud-sprigged fabrics and cushioned wicker. Ben gently laid Jennifer on top of her flounced comforter. The flowers sitting on the end tables on either side of the bed made her feel as though she were spread out in a field of blooms.

Ben stood and pulled off his clothes, then bent tenderly over her. She tried to keep from staring at his enthralling frame, the splendid patterns of hair that curled down from his chest to his loins. Even with his clothes off, his body seemed so mysterious, so private to her.

Slowly, tantalizingly, he undid the jabot of her blouse, then the buttons. "You know, I've always been single-mindedly preoccupied by my work," Ben said with a little quirk to his mouth. "But over the last two weeks, you've been the first thing I've thought about when I wake up and the last thing I think about before I fall asleep." His hands slid inside her blouse and made electric arcs around her breasts, simultaneously unfastening her silken bra.

Jennifer shivered with anticipation, and he made the rest of her clothes slither away from her. He cupped her chin with one hand. His tongue darted in and out of her soft lips, then nipped at them. She duplicated the action, and they fell back against the downy pillows, enfolded.

Ben's palm slid up her outer thigh, which was as smooth as polished alabaster. His touch left little trails of sparks as his hand moved up her taut stomach, then her rib cage to her high breasts. He stopped to trace the stiffened peaks with his fingertips, and she felt passion overcome her with consuming heat. Then his mouth covered the area where his fingers had been. With skillful tongue and teeth he worked at her breasts. She arched her supple back while cradling his head, feeling incredible tenderness toward him.

As Ben kissed the warm nape of her neck she caressed him till he drew in his breath. "Please Ben," she pleaded throatily. "Now. I want you so much."

"No," he said, lightly biting her earlobe. "Not yet . . ."

Jennifer, seething with want, took matters into her own hands and rolled over on top of him. She poised herself there, her thighs tensed in a feline crouch, not taking him, but leaving herself open and ready. Ben's hands moved up to cover her breasts sensuously, and they felt deliciously hot over the sensitive skin. She extended her arms fully above her head.

"Now," she insisted fiercely, "love me." Without warning he arched into her straddled stance. She threw her head back and both her arms dropped. Her fingers drove into his shoulder as they moved together. Their eyes were concentrating on each other's faces and tiny, almost indistinct signals.

As if from far away, Jennifer heard a noise like the roar of the ocean. Then she realized she was hearing the sound of her own heart pounding in her ears. The ecstasy he was giving her mounted, taking her to a delirious height where she was aware of nothing but Ben beneath her. Before she knew it, she was tensing, then shuddering exquisitely. Below her Ben was shaken by the same tremendous force. He stifled a shout.

They seemed frozen for a moment before Jennifer let herself collapse over his hard, tan chest. They kissed and kissed, their hands moving feverishly over one another's skin as if they hadn't gotten enough of each other yet, as if they still wanted to absorb one another.

Finally Jennifer relaxed, letting the top of her curly head curve against Ben's strong neck. "My god," she exclaimed breathlessly, "I never knew that the simple act of just holding someone, all by itself, could be so remarkable."

"Ah, the land of lost content." She felt Ben sigh heavily under her, his chest rising and falling powerfully. "I can't bear being separated from you, Jennifer," he declared, plaintively sincere. "It doesn't feel right. To be apart from you is against nature."

Jennifer thrilled at his words. Again she took in his unique, comfortable smell and let her palm scrape luxuriously against his new growth of beard. "Is that why you came back?" she asked, innocently blissful. "To tell me you can't live without me?"

"Not specifically."

For some reason, icy daggers of dread plunged through her. She lifted her face to stare at her lover, and a cramp of fear distorted her lovely large eyes.

Ben went on heedlessly, "I came to St. Louis to announce that I'm seeking Harris Baker's Senate seat."

Chapter Seven

A number of unpleasant reactions gripped her, foremost among which was a stunned sense of imbalance.

Jennifer decided to handle this as coolly as she was able of. She stirred out of his arms evenly, the way one moves to escape notice from an aroused rattlesnake. "Ben honey," she said in a voice just as affectionate and loving as it had been two minutes earlier, "why haven't you told me?"

"I am telling you." Ben was guileless. "No one else knows about it yet, except the party people who scheduled the press conference tomorrow, when I'll announce my bid."

Jennifer stood up and calmly walked to her closet. She took out a floor-length white satin dressing gown that looked as though it belonged on a forties movie star and slowly looped the sash around her waist. She turned to look at Ben, who was reclining on his side with his head propped up on one arm, covered to the hips by a cotton sheet. The pose made him look incongruously like a beefcake model.

"Would you like to dress and go out to dinner?" he said, unsure of Jennifer's response. "We can talk all about my plans over some Mississippi catfish, if you like."

"Yes, that would be nice." She went into her bathroom to work on her appearance. As she applied makeup and brushed her hair she willed herself not to think, not to make any judgments. She must hear him out. When she reemerged, she saw Ben sitting at the end of the bed fully dressed, pulling on his cowboy boots.

"Ben, maybe it's better that we don't discuss this in a public place," she announced, exhaling.

"Why not?"

"Because this Senate . . . thing is something you know I've been opposed to since we met."

Puzzlement flashed over his features. "You never told me you didn't want me to run." He was right. She had never said directly that she didn't want him to throw his hat in the ring.

Jennifer sat on the edge of a wicker armchair facing him. "Would my objection have been a factor in your decision?" He looked at her unflinchingly without answering, and she fought to control the violent irritation surging up within her. "I'm terribly disappointed that you didn't tell me earlier. After all, you must have been talking this over with all your cronies." Then the frustration slipped out, into her voice. "Yet during all these phone calls of the past two weeks you never confided in me! Don't you trust me?"

"I am confiding in you, here and now." The light in his large azure eyes sputtered like the flame of a candle. "And while I was trying to make my decision, I thought of you constantly. Thinking about you gave me strength, Jennifer, the courage to make the difficult choice . . . because I knew you would stand by me, no matter what."

His words should have placated her immediately. But she was so profoundly, stubbornly, pridefully disappointed that she blotted them out even as he spoke. "Maybe this relationship isn't as complete as I thought, if you won't talk to me," she said briskly, sitting regally straight. "I thought you held me in more esteem than this!"

"Why are you talking this way?" He didn't bother to disguise his exasperation. "You know I love you. You're creating problems! Whatever made you think I wasn't going to run, anyhow?"

"Ever since I've known you, you've been implying that you didn't feel an all-out, fierce aspiration, the *conceit* needed to win. You're just not the type to get in front of a television camera and brag about yourself for an hour, like Senate candidates have to do. And you know it!"

"I had some doubts, but they're only natural."

"Doubts! You said you felt *unworthy* of your elected position."

Ben quietly answered, "I told you I wanted the seat so I could do more for people."

"You led me to assume you weren't going to run," Jennifer cried, feeling like a betrayed child. "I wasn't even sure you were going to run for the House again! What about your ambitions to write? Are you going to kill off that dream just because you're successful in a field where you're not completely happy?"

"Look honey, we're never in as much control of things as we may think we are. Sometimes we just have to accept the role of fate in our lives." Ben idly used a forefinger to brush his upper lip. "I'm a shoo-in for the Senate, right? My party and Mrs. Baker did insist it was my responsibility to run and help maintain the traditional line of power in that party. And after much deliberation, I decided they were right. I owe it to them to run. Not many people ever get the chance to do that." Shrugging, he added, "I've pretty much put my doubts to rest. I can always write when I stop getting reelected. Or when I retire, or choose to stop running. Whatever."

"Do you realize what you're saying?" Jennifer demanded disbelievingly. "You're running because you were pressured to. Because of favors you want to return, because of some sort of political umbilical cord!"

Fuming, Ben said between his teeth, "There was some pressure, but there is no 'umbilical cord.' I want this seat and I'll do my best to win it." His declaration sounded hollow to Jennifer. He went on defensively, "The voters want me. And it's not natural for somebody not to move forward when opportunity beckons with wide-open arms!"

Jennifer knew Ben would never run unless he truly believed he'd make a good senator. As his eyes anxiously searched her face she felt every cell in her body straining toward him. She yearned to shut herself up and hug him and promise to support him all through the upcoming campaign. But another side of her was screaming, I must not love him enough. If I truly loved him I'd accept his decision.

In an appeasing voice Ben said, "I honestly don't see why you're so upset, honey. After all, we've already resolved the conflict-of-interest problem with your editor. Or so you told me."

Suddenly, Jennifer could hold it in no longer. "I

don't want a Senator Benjamin Trostel! I just want Ben!" Her fists clenched and her breast heaved with anxiety.

"What does that mean?" Ben demanded.

Jennifer got up and began pacing. "As a representative, you remain relatively anonymous. You and I could continue without a lot of fuss. But as a senator—damn it, Ben! To win an entire state you become a *product,* a piece of merchandise, packaged to attract consumer attention. You have to star in slick commercials, you're profiled in magazines and newspapers. People are curious about your home life."

"That's part of the job." Ben's eyes had turned to two chunks of blue ice. He obviously was tired of the argument and uncomfortable with having his uncertainties dragged out for him to face again.

He stood up to gaze out the window, his eyes following the traffic, stories below. The line of his mouth was stern. "I'm annoyed and insulted by your objections. Admit that the bottom line of all this is that you don't think I'd make a good senator."

Her reply came slowly, like the letters emerging one by one on an electric billboard. "I think you'd make a great senator. The trouble is, do you?"

The silence in the room was deafening. Earnestly she added, "I instinctively know you wouldn't be happy as a senator, Ben. You won't be true to yourself if you run for the seat."

She'd finally hit a nerve. Ben cringed slightly, since her disturbing words were true. He pivoted. His expression was austere. "And *I* 'instinctively know' that you cannot understand how I have to work for the things I believe in. After all, your job is to sit back and belittle them!"

Jennifer sank to the edge of her bed. "I wondered how long it would take for you to get to that."

He continued, "I knew I was in love with you when your loud criticisms of my profession didn't matter to me. Now I'm beginning to wonder if I can live with that. After all, Senate candidate or not, I'm only myself, and you're not accepting that."

"I don't believe this is happening," Jennifer whispered mournfully, astounded by the force of their anger. "How have we become embattled so quickly? After meeting you at the airport . . . after the love we've made . . ."

Everything she'd ever wanted was being yanked away from her. Their love was slipping away far too easily. She looked up at him abruptly, her brown eyes defiant and her eyebrows lifted. "You know Ben, all this happens to be *your* mistake," she accused petulantly. "*I* haven't done anything objectionable. I'm just an innocent bystander to your problems."

"Name my 'problems.'" His tone of challenge was deadly.

"You didn't discuss with me this poor decision to run for the Senate. I consider that a serious mistake where we're concerned."

"I intended to discuss this with you tonight," he repeated with extreme exasperation.

"But the decision is already made. You were just going to discuss the aftermath with me. And I don't even believe you're fully committed to the decision, no matter how many protestations you make to the contrary. Your lack of dedication is going to create major problems for you." Ben breathed a curse toward his feet, but she went on, "Now I can't believe you've ever had the commitment to me that I made to you!"

"You honestly think that? I guess I can't debate that one away. You'd never let me."

"My god, Ben, I nearly sacrificed my job for you! It's bad enough that my editor knows about us. But with you running for the Senate, every *Herald* reader would find out that the newspaper's editorial cartoonist cozies up to politicians. I could never work effectively with that bad publicity." Though Jennifer wasn't shouting, she was panting with the violent emotions running through her. "What it boils down to is that if you want the Senate race, you can't genuinely want *me*." There was a long, troubling pause.

"I think there's only one problem between us, Jennifer. And that is the fact that you just plain don't like politicians. It's *your* problem, not mine."

"All right, it is mine. And there's no problem with you, of course," she rejoined sarcastically. "You're really quite pleasant . . . when you get your own way."

Right then something came over him. Not resentment, not despair. Rather, his entire bearing and expression became aggressively neutral, colorless. He turned and walked into the living room to pick up his coat. Jennifer followed him.

"I should have stopped this argument right at the start," he said lifelessly. He slid into the leather coat. "But it's best that you said all these things to me now, before our involvement went any further."

His eyes met Jennifer's. She straightened her stance as she regarded the face that had been created for her alone. The air between them dripped with regrets.

She had finally found a man with a will to match her own. But tonight was apparently the last time she would meet it.

"Come tomorrow, I am announcing. If you want to talk more, you know where to get hold of me."

Jennifer stood staring at the door after he'd left. In the space of twenty minutes she'd gone from "the land of lost content" to being a loud critic of politicians. All of her happy plans—even the insignificant little intention to have dinner with David and Lynn Fantle-Johnson—had vanished like wisps of smoke.

"The door has shut on him, not me," she breathed aloud. But she shook with the fear of knowing she'd have to live without the man who had made her life complete.

Chapter Eight

On the last day of February U.S. Representative Benjamin Trostel announced his candidacy with great fanfare and public approval. As March, April and May wore on, endorsements came in from prominent elected officials and public figures. Posters and buttons reading, "Benjamin Trostel: Our Next Great Senator" became as ubiquitous as Coke signs.

Ben Trostel was a winner. And Jennifer was lost without him.

Their last time together, with its abrupt plunge from golden affection to bitter conflict, served as a reminder of how hopeless their relationship would have been had she allowed it to continue, she resolutely told herself. Still, the fact that everything with Ben was over, and that she had personally driven in the killing wedge, left her swimming in despair.

As the winter days tumbled on, Jennifer sharply felt the lack of what she'd known with Ben: the telephone conversations, the sweet shared laughter, the thrilling airport reunions. At times, looking wistfully at the telephone, she imagined that Ben and she were like characters in a melodrama: two people who deserved one another but who destiny kept apart due to circumstances beyond their control.

Despite Jennifer's pain, commonsensical arguments stayed her temptations to call Ben. Had he really loved her, just as she had always wanted? Or had she seen in him the loving qualities that she wanted to see? If he had been the mature, supportive man of her dreams, he would have tried to work things out with her.

In all her broodings, it never occurred to her that she could have tried to work toward him from her side of the street. Instead she wondered if Ben perhaps was simply another one of those men who instantly backed down when things got tough with a woman, a man she shouldn't bother fretting over. How could she ever forge a permanent relationship with a man who wasn't true to himself, who let himself be pressured into running a race he hadn't wanted, body and soul, to enter? Though her brief involvement with a politician had churned her around in a disastrous personal and professional whirlpool, Ben had never budged an inch to change his life-style for her. Unless you wanted to count the phone calls he didn't return while she'd been in Washington with him. She had been the one to make all the compromises, she tried to convince herself. There had been no calming balance or spiritual equality to their affair.

Perhaps Lynn had been right at the very start, when she'd said "that which burns brightest, burns fastest." Everything had been too wonderful, too perfect between Ben and Jennifer. That wasn't long-lasting love; that was an intense affair, an *interlude* whose life span was like that of the brightest meteor in the night sky. Love, when it was the real thing, was firmly based, solid and stable, she decided. Stable, if a little duller, perhaps, than what she'd known with Ben.

Jennifer's nervous depression only fueled her work. Her drawings and humor were never more trenchant. Every night before bed she swam laps in the pool on the top floor of her condominium building to calm her nerves. Her body quickly acquired more tone and her skin acquired a certain pearly translucence. She didn't notice.

The one time Jennifer tried to contact Ben was an unmitigated disaster. On a Friday in late April she read that he was making an appearance at a St. Louis labor meeting over the weekend. She knew he would probably be spending some time at his local apartment. Staring out her office window at the glaring morning sunshine, she remembered how oddly welcome she had felt in that barren, unlived-in space, just because it was Ben's.

I'm lonely for him, she acknowledged as the morning turned into afternoon. The feeling has just gotten stronger with time; it won't leave me. I can't eat or sleep without thinking about him. He couldn't possibly miss me in the same way. He would have contacted me if he were lonely for me. He isn't as stubborn as I am. Maybe he is. I can't remember.

At some point after lunch the pride in her head melted into the longing inside her heart. Jennifer found herself looking into a mirror, checking her appearance as carefully as if she were about to meet Ben for a date. The gesture meant that she was subconsciously planning on talking to him, she surmised. It was an omen that she must bring herself to do something she had always assumed she'd never do.

An omen! More like an excuse, Jennifer taunted herself silently as she looked at the phone. It squatted on her office desk like a nasty little creature. Resolving once and for all to call Ben's apartment, she willed herself to accept the consequences.

"Damn the torpedoes, full speed ahead," she muttered as she punched the phone dial with stiff fingers. She squeezed the handset as if bravely forcing herself not to hang up.

The line rang twice. When the receiver was picked up at the other end, she felt a happiness radiate through her chest. Then she heard: "Hello?"

A woman's voice. Sultry, low, melodic.

Jennifer gulped silently. The woman repeated, "Hello? Who is this?" After a pause, the woman hung up and the phone clicked off.

Only for an instant did Jennifer wonder if she'd reached the wrong number. She had definitely dialed Ben's local place. She felt herself swallowed up by a jealous fury as she replaced the receiver. Her mood descended completely from one of reconciliation to vicious anger. Pure, undiluted spite prickled at her as she picked up the day's newspaper. Ben sure hadn't needed much time to recover from their breakup. She was all alone, and he was not. "He'll pay for this," she swore. She was amazed by this unfamiliar childish rage. At the same time she could not suppress it.

In a way she was relieved that his new girl friend had answered. At least it had immediately let her know what was what. Surely the woman was Ben's companion, if he allowed her the intimacy of picking up his home phone. If he had answered, there would have been the sad, awkward explanation of his involvement, followed by the inevitable standard phrase, "Well, hope to see you around."

Plans for vengeance were forming inside her head without her even being fully aware of it. She leafed quickly through the newspaper till she found what she was looking for.

A small photograph of Representative Benjamin Trostel arrested her gaze. Every time she'd seen his picture, she felt the warmth of his skin and breath, seen the sparkle of his blue eyes. She could almost touch that face. She'd missed it. She wouldn't anymore. Accompanying the picture was a news item on his not showing up to vote for a public-works bill that would indirectly benefit northeastern Missouri. "In many ways I wanted to vote for it, since it would have some positive effects for state residents," he told the reporter. "But it's unnecessarily costly, and I don't believe in pork-barrel projects, so I am ambivalent on the issue. The best thing for me to do for our St. Louis district was not to vote."

Jennifer tossed the paper aside. In a flurry of emotion she began sketching Ben sitting astride a wooden fence. This time, she overexaggerated the well-known features—the big eyes, the large white smile, the casualness in dress. She wrote "public-works bill" on the fence. The caption she penciled over the picture read, "Have Fence, Will Straddle." She put the rough sketch in an envelope and had Darlene, the receptionist, take it to Frank Quarters.

A half hour later Frank came to her office declaring,

"I thought we hashed this out! Ben Trostel is off limits to you Jenny, and that's that." Standing in front of her desk, he shook his head and added, "It's excellent and I'm dying to use it, but it's conflict of interest. Even if the two of you have called it quits."

Surprise was written all over Jennifer's face. "How did you know?"

"You've looked down in the mouth ever since Trostel announced for the Senate. It wasn't too hard to figure out what's happened."

"It's true," she confessed, shamefaced. "After all the compromising you did for me, we found out we had problems *we* couldn't compromise about."

Frank grunted. "I could have told you it wouldn't last. A politician and a political skeptic mix together like oil and water. What disappoints me is that you wanted to use your cartoon space as a spot for you to grind your ax."

"Come on, Frank. Now that my time with Ben is through, I may as well resume covering all issues. You like the cartoon, why not let it fly? It's timely and well balanced. It's a good opinion. It belongs in the paper."

Frank looked out the window for a minute, then back at Jennifer. His look was one of concession.

"All right"—he sighed—"if this sticks in Trostel's craw, that's his problem. Do up the final drawing, we'll go with it."

Jennifer tried to keep the petty glee out of her tone. "Thank you."

"By the way, I'm sorry things went the way they did between you two."

"I am, too," Jennifer said distractedly. Her mind

was already on the task at hand. This will get to Ben, she thought repeatedly as she sketched away. If nothing else does, this will get to him.

"Have Fence, Will Straddle" was one of the most popular cartoons the *Herald* published that year. But when it appeared the following Wednesday, Jennifer tearfully told Lynn Fantle-Johnson, "I'm so ashamed of myself! It was like the sweet taste of revenge to draw it, but now my pettiness is out in the open for the world to see. All I've done is prove that I'm the most vindictive person in St. Louis."

"Jenny, the cartoon just isn't that vicious," Lynn said sympathetically. "All you wanted to do was get Ben's attention, not goad him or cut him down."

"If there'd been the tiniest chance for a reunion, that cartoon has shot a silver bullet right through that chance!"

"That's not necessarily true. Love makes us all do crazy, uncontrollable things. Ben knows that as well as anyone, I'm sure. He probably knows exactly what you're going through."

Jennifer found no hope in what Lynn was saying. She smiled sadly. "Worst of all, I've abused my position to take a cheap shot at someone."

"It's not a cheap shot, it's a good, funny cartoon!"

"I guess I'll benefit from this experience, at any rate. It's been a lesson."

When Jennifer opened her mailbox on Friday, there was a cream parchment envelope inside. She nearly dropped it when she saw the return insignia was that of U.S. Representative Benjamin Trostel.

"Hate mail," she murmured through thickened lips. "Nothing less than what I deserve."

Jennifer went upstairs, her heart heavy. Inside her apartment she sat down on the suede couch without removing her raincoat. The envelope was still gripped in her hand, unopened. Jennifer switched on the light. Swallowing her breath, she began to tear open the seal with trembling fingers. A strange sort of terrified curiosity engulfed her as she unfolded the letter. The "Representative" had been crossed off the letterhead, as he had always done with previous communications to her.

"Dear Jennifer," Ben had started with his loopy handwriting, "I'm pleased to see that you can do cartoons on me again. There's no one I'd rather have caricature my admitted 'fence-straddling.' Although I liked the drawing very much (unlike my cringing aides), I don't believe I'll request the original *this* time.

"The cleverness behind your work only emphasizes how much I miss Jennifer Aldrich and what she brought into my life.

"I know I've hurt you. I realize now I could have talked to you earlier about the decision to run for the Senate. But your response wasn't exactly a love-tap reminder of that fact. The urgency of campaign decisions always creates ripples of bad timing and hasty reactions.

"As I said before, you know where to reach me."

He'd signed it, "Ben."

Her eyes devoured the brief note several times over. Then her fingers splayed open limply and the paper drifted to the floor with the dry rustle of an autumn leaf. She was profoundly disappointed. Why had he even bothered to send this? She could not read any deep-seated, heartfelt sincerity behind the words. He said, "I miss you," but he didn't apologize. He feebly attempted to explain away his willfull tardiness in telling her about jumping into the senate race. That was it. He said she could call him, not that he would call her. And he had not said, "I love you."

Jennifer closed her wet, brown eyes in pain and rested her head back against the couch. She'd hoped he would make a stronger attempt than this to straighten things out. The very shallowness of his message indicated that he didn't fervently want her back. Too many things kept them apart, and a fainthearted letter didn't even start to mend it all.

The way she felt, though, any message would have been too late. Jennifer didn't want to be led back into the same situation in which they'd been embroiled before. She wasn't going to try to resurrect a love that hadn't been the real thing in the first place.

It would be best not to act on this letter at all. Their interlude had ended in February. Time for her to acknowledge completely that an episode in her life was over.

Additional communication from Ben was not forthcoming. Though Jennifer couldn't fully deny she wanted him to get in touch with her, she didn't expect him to. At the start of May her heart was unexpectedly gladdened by a call from the executive editor of her newspaper syndicate.

"We're looking for a new comic strip for our lineup," Mr. Agnelli told her from the main office in Chicago. "Something contemporary that will comment on political, social, cultural issues, all highly topical. And we want it scathingly funny. We've been studying your work for a long time, and we want you to take a crack at it. Interested?"

Jennifer hadn't felt such enthusiasm in months. A comic strip would be a challenge, and it could be fun. And extremely lucrative. "How soon do you want to see something?"

Not long after she replaced the phone, Jennifer found herself involuntarily mulling over Ben again. Even if she'd been offered such a comic strip a year ago and had not been strictly a political cartoonist when she met him, the old conflict-of-interest problem still would have arisen between them. Given the focus of a topical comic strip on hot political and economic events, even if she didn't criticize Ben in particular, she would still necessarily have been lampooning his colleagues. His peers would have avoided him like the plague because of his companion's touchy profession.

The whole idea only reiterated to Jennifer how hopeless the affair with Ben had been all along, and how disastrous it would have been in the end if allowed to continue. She needed every straw she could grasp at in the constant struggle to persuade herself that she was no longer in love with Ben Trostel.

The first Monday in June, Jennifer called Mr. Agnelli with her concept. "My comic strip would be set within the environs of a newspaper," she proposed. "The characters could be journalists, and we could follow them to Washington, New York, the Middle East—wherever the news is being made."

"Sounds good, I like it," Agnelli returned pleasantly. "How 'bout sketching up about twenty sample panels? You've got a little while; we don't need to see them till August or so." He took time to explain that the price each publication would pay for her strip would depend on its popularity and how much the buyer wanted it. Large publications with high circulations paid three times as much as smaller outlets. "Feature syndication is the last frontier of supply and demand," Agnelli concluded for her.

Elated, Jennifer called Lynn's desk to see if she wanted to be taken out to a celebratory lunch. Lynn squealed with a delight that the occasion didn't really merit, then suggested a certain restaurant downtown. "Let's go as soon as possible!" she insisted, puzzling Jennifer with her excessive enthusiasm.

As she got up to leave she scanned her copy of the morning *Herald*, and the solid, cold steel bar of pain that had lodged in her heart tingled sharply for just an instant. The front-page headline splashed over Ben Trostel's photograph read TROSTEL ASSUMES BAKER MANTLE WITH CONFIDENCE, NEW IMAGE. The article reviewed his endorsement victory at his party's state convention just two days earlier. On her way out the door Jennifer threw the paper into the recycling bin.

Though Jennifer looked a little work-worn in her khaki-colored linen dress, her spirits were high as she and Lynn strode briskly to downtown St. Louis's most popular spot for lunch. The streets were flooded with the buttery light of the summer sun as people hurried along the sidewalks, self-conscious and neat in their crisp business clothes.

Lynn was making Jennifer laugh as they headed for the restaurant's double doors. "Just wait," she declared. "In a few years we'll be seeing paperback reprints of your strip, animated TV specials by Jennifer Aldrich, key rings with your cartoon characters, sheets and towels, nightlights, video arcade games—"

"Stop it," Jennifer protested breathlessly as she reached for a chrome door handle. "You're getting me all worked up."

Abruptly Lynn's high-cheekboned face seemed to freeze. She was looking at something over Jennifer's head.

Jennifer whirled and found herself standing face to chest with Ben Trostel. He was coming out of the restaurant as she was going in.

Her jaw dropped. She literally felt her knees shaking. Ben looked unable to move. This was the first time they'd seen each other in person since the winter. They stood there, gazing blatantly at one another. His eyes were an electric blue between their black, straight lashes, his skin golden tan. Passersby could read with a glance the radiance of the passion flowing between them.

Jennifer was shocked at how Ben already looked distinctly senatorial. His three-piece suit and silk tie were perfect, combining fit and style and worn with an authority she'd never seen on him before. The fawn-colored hair was neatly styled. He looked tall and stoic, and he still looked as though he'd been formed for Jennifer alone.

"How are you?" he said at last with half a smile. He seemed totally unaware of Lynn's presence.

"Fine. And you?"

"Not bad. Jennifer . . ."

At that moment a leggy woman came up from behind Ben. Her carriage expressed a certain quality and breeding. She laid a proprietary hand over his shoulder and in a deep, musical voice inquired, "Ben, darling, who are these people?"

Her familiar voice cut Jennifer like a knife. It was the same woman who had answered the phone in his apartment.

Chapter Nine

Ben finally came to life, and he brought his diplomat's skills into play. He grinned and took the woman's wrist, saying easily, "Lynn Fantle-Johnson, Jennifer Aldrich, I want you to meet my campaign manager, Karen McAvoy. Karen, of course, you know Lynn from the newspaper, and Jennifer is the *Herald*'s cartoonist."

"I see. How good to meet you at last, Jennifer," Karen said warmly, her hazel eyes suddenly surrounded with friendly crinkles. She was at least a decade older than Ben. "I've admired your work for quite a while."

"Thank you," Jennifer replied. She couldn't help but notice the wide gold wedding band on Karen's left hand. She was married, a business friend of Ben's, and her sultry voice now sounded quite nice to Jennifer's ears.

Ben turned to Jennifer, and a familiar tension hummed between them. As they regarded each other in the resplendent summer air every speck of bitterness they'd felt toward one another faded away. He took her hands in both of his, and a sensation shot right through her.

"Congratulations on your endorsement," she said dutifully.

"I'm busy congratulating myself on running into you again," he responded. He squeezed her fingers, then said regretfully, "We've got to go." He leaned down to kiss her lightly on the cheek. The touch of his lips was pleasantly cool. She sighed. He smelled as clean and fresh as she remembered.

Jennifer briefly observed Ben as he sauntered down the sunny walk with Karen. The familiar sight of his straight, lanky frame nearly mesmerized her. She shook herself and turned to Lynn, whose coal eyes glinted mischievously. She accused, "All right, how did you manage to set up this little 'chance encounter'?"

Lynn erupted with triumphant giggling. "I was on the phone with Ben a little while ago, asking him some questions for my story tomorrow. He excused himself by saying he had to meet his campaign manager for lunch at this place. Then you called, and I decided to create a little story of my own."

"But so much has happened between us. So much time has passed! You matchmaker! What if we'd have hurled thunderbolts and lightning at each other?"

"You two *are* lightning together." Lynn smirked. "There was no risk involved. After all, Jenny, several times when I've been questioning Trostel he's asked about you. It was assumed that I couldn't relay his concern—confidentiality and reporter-source relations, you understand! And you've been pining over Ben for months, despite your too-vigorous denials."

"I wonder what will happen now," Jennifer said wistfully. She was still so dazed that she stumbled a little as she entered the crowded restaurant.

"He'll call, of course," Lynn stated flatly. "I stood

there and watched our next great senator turn to stone. No man is going to let a prize like you slip through his fingers twice."

A watched phone *does* ring, Jennifer discovered a few hours later. After lunch she sat doodling restlessly at her desk, pridefully unwilling to use the phone herself but still waiting for Ben to phone her. A couple of times the phone jangled, but each time it was another *Herald* employee. Each time she let it ring several times before answering with a studiedly casual "Yes?" Both times her eyes stung with disappointment when the voice on the other end did not belong to Ben.

At four-thirty, the phone rang again. This time she immediately grabbed the receiver with a near-frantic "Hello?"

"It's me, Jennifer."

Relief and longing washed over her like a wave. "Oh Ben, I'm so glad you called."

His voice was hushed and a little apprehensive. "I'd like to see you."

"I want to see you, too. I've learned to *adore* politicians. Even those with ... 'bad timing'."

"And I've learned a few things too." Ben chuckled, a warm sound Jennifer had heard often in her imagination. "You *did* get my letter. Why didn't you call me?"

Feeling silly, Jennifer said, "Because I *had* called your St. Louis place. Karen answered, I think. That beautiful voice of hers convinced me you were working on a playboy senator image!"

Ben laughed heartily. "No, sunshine, I've been too busy campaigning to take anybody out. And, Jennifer, no one has interested me since you and I . . . I want to take you out again, badly. Do you have anything going tonight? Are you free for dinner?"

"Oh, Ben, yes," she breathed in reply. She'd be seeing him again. Hearing him. Touching him.

"Dinner at eight, then. I'll swing by your place."

When Jennifer replaced the phone, a small smile was on her lips. She left work early to have her hair cut. The early summer sun had already brought out some light auburn highlights, and her curls were increasingly longish and haphazard.

"No cut!" the hairdresser insisted when she climbed into his chair. "Just a trim!" Relying on his judgment, Jennifer left the salon with loose curls tumbling romantically around her shoulders. At home she applied her makeup with meticulous care. But she didn't need to apply the glow that had been on her small face since she'd encountered Ben. The fragility of her look was not diminished by the halter-top dress she put on, made of black mousseline and appliquéd with gold lamé lilies.

Jennifer slipped into her thin, black silk sandals before circling her living room to light the many candles that had been dark for so long. Did she truly want him back? For months she had been telling herself she did not, always knowing her real feelings. The security system buzzed just as she blew out the match.

Warily Jennifer surveyed the large main room, illuminated by candles and a spot over her prized Klee lithograph. She critically reevaluated herself in the vermeil-framed foyer mirror, and saw how her shoulders and arms reflected the gleam of the dramatic lighting.

The knock at the door startled her. As she opened it, Ben's finely-carved mouth spread into a smile of pure delight. He wore a formal navy pinstripe suit that made his eyes look darker. "Please come in," she said softly.

He slammed the door behind him and took Jennifer in his arms urgently. He pressed his lips against her face and mouth repeatedly, his kisses feeling like a rain of falling stars against her warm skin. She pressed herself to him as though she'd just been released from bondage, and she had: her heart was flying free, like a great bird that has escaped its cage. He rubbed his big hands over her bare back, and she gasped at the coolness of his palms on her smooth skin.

"Let's sit down and talk before we go, shall we?" Ben said. Drawing her to his side, he walked her to the long couch and nestled her close to him.

"Nothing has changed." He sighed happily. "That much is clear."

"You've changed," Jennifer accused. "You look so dignified and stately. You used to be rather . . . casual."

"You mean sloppy."

She pursed her lips, frowning. "No. You look severe, like you mean business—and rather sexy."

"I'm glad you think so." He laughed. "My party told me to clean up and stop running around looking like a farmhand. I was ordered never to be seen publicly without this Turnbull and Asser rig, in hopes the voters will forget I'm an immature thirty-two."

"Thirty-two?"

"I had a birthday last month. Time marches on." Ben looked Jennifer up and down again appreciatively before kissing the end of her little nose. "But it's pretty obvious that time, and distance, and one devastating spat, haven't gotten in the way of what we feel."

"Ben, I love you still," Jennifer confessed awkwardly, eyes down. "While we were apart, I forced myself to think it wasn't *real* before. None of it. Now I know I'm wrong." She lifted her face to him hesitantly. "And I don't think you're a fence-straddler! I drew that cartoon to get your attention, and begged my editor to print it. I wouldn't have used such a pathetic 'get your goat' ploy if I hadn't loved you." She shook her head slowly, in sad wonderment. "I still don't understand why I argued with you like I did, and allowed things to end there."

"I do." Ben shifted and laid the weight of her head on his shoulder. One hand reached up to stroke her curls languidly while the other remained interlaced with hers. "We are two complex, relatively settled persons. You and I have been alone, separate, for so many years, establishing our well-ordered little lives, becoming selfish about our individuality. In my own way, I think I've become a snake who wasn't ready, at least not then, to shed his old protective skin." Before them a candle flame fluttered, then steadied.

"So when someone comes along—namely yourself—and starts dissolving that skin for the first time, I got scared and looked for any excuse to jump ship without being aware of my own fear. I think we were both looking for some kind of fault." As he spoke Jennifer remembered with searing clarity how she first had been frightened when she realized that Ben was the man meant for her to love. "Romance does require its own kind of bravery. So our first argument was a convenient excuse for us to split and avoid those troubling implications about the depth of our feelings."

She roused herself and spoke about the cause of

their breakup for the first time. "But Ben, your decision about the Senate is a real problem."

"Another couple could have talked about it without parting ways in a colossal snit! Let's face it, we hadn't known each other long enough to handle it. In retrospect, that quick argument seems ridiculous, nothing more than the senseless ravings of two people who hadn't had enough time to know each other fully. We needed more opportunities to know the other better, and deeper. We didn't know it, but were scared of each other. Both of us. And too proud to rush back together when our best instincts begged for it."

Jennifer, looking at him, wondered at how well he knew her. He had such a full, strong, clear understanding of her. She breathed in his scent, blended with the burning of the sandalwood candles. "I'm not afraid now. Are you?" Her hands moved inside his jacket to stroke him richly, expressively.

"Who, me?" Ben murmured affectionately. "Not of you," he said as he tentatively kissed her temple. "Nor of being in love," he continued, nipping at her earlobe and making a shiver run through her petite frame, "as long as I know you love me." He took her hopeful face between both of his hands. Jennifer lowered her eyelids as he said, "Our brief relationship was too perfect. We can have it back again now, don't you agree?"

With her chin still dropped, she looked up at him, striking him with the full impact of her wide, brown gaze. "Oh, yes."

Their lips joined. At that instant, any last barrier standing between them fell away, vanquished like a slain enemy. Their arms tightened as their mouths opened to each other, tongues boldly rediscovering soft, pliant territory. Jennifer arched her back as Ben drew her even closer, his arms nearly crossed at the elbow where they pulled against her back. They shared kisses with dreams in them, kisses full of life.

Ben leaned back to watch his hands glide from the mold of her Jennifer's neck, over her shoulders until his palms rested over her breasts. His touch burned her right through the mousseline.

"This dress is wonderful. But I'd like it off you. I want to see you again. All of you."

Jennifer smiled knowingly as she stood up. With grave care Ben unfastened the halter neck of her dress. With a whooshing sound, he pulled it over her head and tossed it on the couch like a discarded flower. She pushed off his jacket and went through the elaborate ritual of undoing his vest, then shirt buttons. With each instant, the pull of passion grew stronger and quicker between them, like a living object. Before she had finished undressing him, she moved her hand over the place of his hardening desire while her other arm encircled him at the small of his back. They stood close together, outlined in the glow of the candlelight, and it was impossible to tell where his aura began and hers left off.

Ben's savoring gaze traveled to Jennifer's bare breasts, which made curved shadows above her tapering ribs and small waist, taunting him with their closeness. Her fingers raked his light brown hair as his damp mouth closed over her aroused, hardening nipples. The slow, rough sweeping of his tongue and teeth over the pulsating points of skin made her sigh blissfully and smile in a way she never had before. Every part of her was tingling and alive, purring with a want for him.

She felt such love and happiness and desire that she wanted him to take her as soon as possible, but she didn't protest when he dropped to his knees. He seemed to be examining her splendidly shaped thighs. "You look better than ever, if that's possible," he said in a low voice. His hand traveled slowly, slowly up the inside of her smooth, soft leg. "There's a sheen to your skin I didn't notice before."

The swimming, she remembered, thanking herself for her nightly regimen. She couldn't continue thinking then as Ben's hand reached inside the shiny jet satin of her panties. He lingered, then gently pulled the slithery material until she was completely nude. His supple, gentle fingers were as insubstantial as mist as they slid deep inside her, awakening her further. At the same time he covered one jutting hipbone with a blizzard of kisses. Jennifer looked down at his tousled head, feeling joyful, gentle emotion as he continued his caressing exploration.

Suddenly she sucked in her breath as his hands reached around to claim her yielding, sensitized hindquarters. His mouth and tongue launched into the most private part of her. All of her feelings gathered and concentrated at the crest of a tidal wave as Ben took his time exquisitely ravishing her.

She let herself build and hang on the edge, mastering her senses. She felt him reach for her shoulders and pull her down under him on the softness of the sheepskin rug.

"The bedroom—" she offered feebly before she found herself hotly kissing his impassioned face, his strong neck. She relished the hardness of his body as she stretched under him. "It's been so long." She sighed.

"So long?" Ben returned huskily. "It seems like

forever. But you make it worth the wait, I swear." As he surged himself into her he murmured, "I love you." Jennifer tenderly curved one cool palm over the taut, feverish skin of his cheek and repeated the phrase.

This time their lovemaking was a very conscious, shared experience in the plentitude of love, much slower and even more intense than the passion they'd known in the winter. After their joining they clung together on the plush rug as the golden candlelight continued playing over their glistening bodies. Their flesh radiated with a supernatural heat as they touched each other carefully, as if the other would break under their feather-light caresses.

Jennifer had never seen a look of contentment as complete as the one on Ben's handsome, darkly tan face at this moment. His index finger traced the line of her jaw as he wonderingly said, "I've never fully realized before how making love can have so many different meanings."

"And what is the meaning of that?" She smiled. She was glad they hadn't gone into the bedroom. Here on the massive white rug, it actually felt as though they were floating on a self-contained cloud of tenderness and love, a soft haven not yet discovered by other humans.

"Well," he began with a slight smile, "lovemaking can be definite communication. For instance, right now, you and I have become 'reacquainted'—"

"That's putting it mildly," she muttered against his neck.

He gave her a look of mock sternness, and went on, "and we've just forgiven each other everything, we've reestablished everything we've felt about one another. And . . ."

In his pause Jennifer heard a distant symphony. She inhaled with anticipation.

"And I think we've just proved that our love is forever," he finished. She rolled over on him, clasped her hands behind his neck and began kissing him rapturously.

Suddenly she remembered a bit of the world that existed outside the room. "Ben," she cried, "what about the restaurant?"

Unhurriedly he reached for his watch. "We're way overdue for our reservation. How about that?" A lazy grin spread across his face.

Jennifer smiled conspiratorially. "So the maître d' will never speak to you again."

"One less vote for Senator Trostel." Ben shrugged. And he smiled at her, the same way he had smiled at her when he first encountered her on the street on that same remarkable day.

Chapter Ten

Jennifer looked neither to the left nor the right as she entered the French bistro the following evening. She anticipated Ben's striking presence, and blazed with joy when she saw him in an out-of-the-way nook. He was sitting under an old wall clock, with a swinging brass pendulum and murals of the French countryside.

He signaled enthusiastically when he saw her, then stood, displaying a lanky figure in cotton tweed, and kissed her possessively before allowing her to sit and catch her breath.

"So, this is how a candidate for the Senate behaves in public!" she exclaimed.

"And this is how you look in the summer!" Ben indicated her white jacket with pinched sleeves, worn over a dress shaped like an elongated T-shirt. With her dark brown-and-auburn curls and smoldering eyes, she looked fantastically alluring. "You look even more beautiful now than you did in the winter. I didn't think that possible." As if he couldn't help himself, he leaned over and repeatedly kissed her cheek with little butterfly touches that made her shiver deliciously.

As he sat back Jennifer was secretly glad that they

had a corner all to themselves. Discretion. Privacy. Freedom to be alone together and to enjoy gourmet food at the same time. Though they continued to stare into each other's eyes, the waiter apparently thought it was finally safe to take their order and appeared at the table. Ben called for Dover sole and Chateaubriand, sauce bearnaise, sweetbreads and raspberries with thick cream. Throughout the meal, they discussed his campaign and her burgeoning career in cartooning. He was very proud that her syndicate had asked her to propose a comic strip.

After they were done spooning down their voluptuous raspberries, Jennifer found herself gazing fondly at Ben again. He looked fiercely handsome in the soft, coppery lighting. "You have such a perfect face," she said helplessly.

"Only to you and my mother," he countered, grinning.

"I'd love to talk over your face with your mother. I'd love to have her tell me about you when you were a little boy, in fact. I'd like to see your baby pictures." Jennifer rested her chin on a fist. "I find everything about you fascinating, Ben. I want to know everything about you."

"I've been waiting for you to make such a request." He was quite serious.

"You mean, you want me to meet your mother?"

"I want you to meet my mother, I want to take you home." He paused. "Jennifer, I want to marry you."

The night sang. A mist dropped over her eyes as her heart melted. Marriage. It was the word she'd always craved to hear but hadn't dared think about. She wanted to marry Ben more than anything in the world. But she was practical . . .

Or at least she was for several moments.

"Jennifer, darling, don't you want to get married?"

She looked to his concerned eyes, and the yearning on her face deepened. "Of course I do. I love you. I know just how incomplete my life is without you. Only . . . but . . ."

"But?" he asked expectantly.

"What about our professions? I've thought about it and thought about it, and they're absolutely incompatible. Have you envisioned being a senator saddled with a wife who draws spiteful lampoons of his colleagues? Your peers would act mighty edgy around you. You might even be ostracized by the people you have to work with. And wouldn't the two of us be a fine pair on the Washington social scene! Your closest colleagues would say, 'Here comes that nice Trostel fella with his bitchy wife who draws those vicious cartoons about me.' How effective can you be as a senator then?"

He rubbed his jaw thoughtfully, as though he'd never considered these possibilities. He didn't interrupt Jennifer as she continued, "A politician's wife never risks open disagreement with her spouse on any subject. As a cartoonist or comic strip artist I'd probably be doing that to you constantly, for the entire nation to see! I don't think voters would consider me a fitting wife. Nor would your party."

"I'm willing to risk that," Ben countered firmly. "But you're forgetting the advantages you'd have as a political wife. No matter where we live, I'll always have to be on prolonged trips. You're independent. You have your own important, vital job. You wouldn't give a damn how late I'd get home. And best of all, as somebody involved in politics—in your own way, that is—we could share everything."

It was all true. Still, Jennifer was realistic enough to know how her career could hurt Ben's. Hesitantly she said, "If worse came to worse, I could give up my work. I love you enough to do that, Ben."

He laughed disparagingly. "If you did that, Sunshine, you'd be the biggest romantic since the Duke of Windsor. I know it would be impossible for you to walk away from your job and take up something less exciting."

The waiter came up to take their orders for an after-dinner drink, then vanished. Ben leaned forward with his elbows on the table and steepled his fingers. He said carefully, "Did you ever stop to consider that I might not make it into the Senate?"

Jennifer was aghast. "You mean lose the election! You're a shoo-in, Ben! As Harris Baker's protégé you've got it made!"

"Shoo-ins," he flatly stated, "don't always get in."

She sat frozen, virtually in shock, as he began reciting a litany of reasons why he might lose the race. The opposition had "targeted" the Baker Senate seat, and they were going to use all the money and resources available to defeat Baker's proposed successor. Ben's opponent, Walter B. Williams, a middle-aged corporate president, was proving to be tough competition.

"But the newspaper poll shows that you're far ahead of Williams," Jennifer pointed out.

"The margin is tighter in the party's secret polls," Ben cautioned. He sighed heavily. "This is going to be a tough race, much more difficult than I thought. Many times I find myself wishing I'd stayed in the House. I also find myself wishing I hadn't run for anything. But everyone I knew was pushing me to get in there for Harris and the party. If I hadn't thrown my hat in the ring, I would have earned some very nasty enemies in every sphere of influence in the country."

Jennifer was not about to snap "I told you so" at this point. She dared to say, "And if you *do* lose . . ."

"Then I'll be free to do some of the things I've always wanted to do. I was born to be a writer, Jennifer; I was *made* to be a politician. So even if I lose the race I win, right?"

"Yes."

"Make no mistake," he said sternly, "I *will* be senator. All things considered, the party has no true doubt about it."

She felt his sudden enthusiasm was more for himself than for her. His tone was sunnier as he continued. "But just in case Williams does win the election, I guess I can do anything my heart desires. I'm no spendthrift, babe. I've been lucky with my investments over the years. I'm comfortably off."

"As a future bride, that's comforting to know," Jennifer said with a wry smile.

Undiluted pleasure filled Ben's face. "That's right! I nearly forgot that I made a marriage proposal tonight."

"You did not forget!" She was so buoyant she marveled at her ability to stay earthbound. She was about to speak, but their drinks arrived. Picking up her glass by the stem she went on, nearly whispering, "I've loved you and wanted you since we've first met, Ben. I have to be bound to you, inextricably. Nothing less will do. But as you said last night, we're both set in our ways. Look at how I resisted letting my heart become fully intertwined with yours! I'm not some malleable, submissive young girl anymore. Are you willing to work with me and my rigid ways?"

Tears, coming out of nowhere, had beaded her eyelashes. Ben reached to touch them with the tips of his fingers, and the drops disappeared as he did so. "I'd be so honored to have you and your alleged rigid ways. As a younger girl, you might have merely yielded to my proposal with no sense of what your decision really meant. But at the age of twenty-seven, you're making a deliberate choice."

She laughed lightly and picked up one of his large, warm hands to press against the side of her luminous face.

"I suppose we should make tentative plans," Ben said caressingly.

"Maybe plans to make plans. Let's keep things secret until after the election, all right? I don't want to disturb the momentum of your campaign."

"We'll let the world know in November, then."

It was as though Ben's heart were shining right through his golden face, his love plainly advertised.

Jennifer sat enchanted, admiring her future husband. A man unafraid of showing his emotions, yet strong and proud, always in command. Very intelligent, versatile, romantic, passionate ... with a touch of stubbornness that made him quite human.

She was boundlessly thrilled at the prospect of marrying him. Looking at him, for the first time she knew all things were possible.

Chapter Eleven

"Mix 'n match politics," stated the caption under the newspaper photo of Ben and Jennifer. "Rep. Benjamin Trostel took a break from his Senate campaign Sunday to stroll through Shaw Gardens with his friend, *Herald* political cartoonist Jennifer Aldrich. Aldrich stopped drawing cartoons about Trostel soon after she met him, citing 'conflict of interest.'"

The dying days of my privacy have started, Jennifer thought with despair as she studied the *Herald*'s photograph of the couple inside the Climatron greenhouse. It was a month after their secret engagement. In between Ben's campaign swings across the state and commutes to the capital, they were able to spend roughly one night together out of seven. He swore that their fleeting visits made his grueling schedule all worth it.

Every day she received Ben's calls from Missouri towns large and small: Jefferson City, Palmyra, Vienna, Blodgett, and other towns she'd never heard of. He spoke at political rallies and fund-raising dinners all over the state. He was constantly quoted in the press and most of the media implied support of him. His popularity ranked higher than ever, according to every poll. His opponent Walter B. Williams, who was outspending him two to one, called him "Blue-eyed Baby Ben" to put down both his eye-catching appearance and his relative youthfulness.

When Ben would show up at Jennifer's place, sometimes without warning, he was always exhausted by the rigors of his week on the road. A few hours spent with her seemed to thoroughly rejuvenate him, though. It made her realize fully how much he needed her.

Last weekend they'd made it to Shaw Gardens. They had come to stand behind a grove of hothouse flowers and had been laughing over some shared witticism. The smiles on their faces had crumpled when they had heard the camera click. Jennifer had looked up to see Mark Reid, one of the *Herald*'s staff photographers.

"Mark," she'd cried, "what are *you* doing here?"

"To paraphrase your own work," he'd answered with a wily grin, "have camera, will travel. I take it everywhere. You never know when that next great photo is going to occur!"

"If it turns out," Ben offered, "I'd like to buy one."

"Matte or glossy?" Mark returned with a wink.

It had turned out, and the *Herald*'s editors had printed it with a threefold purpose, Jennifer surmised: it had news value, human interest value and the caption indirectly emphasized how the *Herald*'s cartoonist's work was untainted by her personal life.

Though she despised the publicity, Jennifer couldn't help but love Mark's candid photograph. It made Ben and her look young, attractive, absorbed in each other, happy, successful and altogether rather enviable. She cut it out of the paper and pinned it on the bulletin board next to her desk, then sat and wistfully gazed at the two of them.

It seemed to her that she and Ben, together, had created another entity. There was Ben, and there was Jennifer, and then there was Ben and Jennifer. The two of them combined made something bigger and better, as though one and one equaled three. And baby makes four? she speculated mirthfully.

Some time later, while she was working on the day's cartoon, the phone rang. The caller was Bobby Bettman, an overly intense aide on Ben's campaign. She'd met him twice, each time feeling his vibrations of thinly veiled contempt.

"Hey, short stuff," he started too jovially, "how's it hangin'?"

He's calling me "short stuff" to keep me in my place, Jennifer thought with irritation. Playing his game, she returned oh so sweetly, "Bobby, how lovely to hear from you. What can I do for you?"

"Nothing for me"—he guffawed—"but you could do a lot for the party by quitting your lambasting of the governor! After all, this is a reelection year."

"Gee Bobby, I'm sorry," Jennifer drawled. "But the governor only gets what he deserves." She chuckled tactfully.

"No, what I'm really calling to ask is ... don't you have a little more influence around that joint?" Jennifer's silence demanded further explanation, and Bobby continued, "Couldn't you have stopped that picture from running? I mean, it doesn't look good for The Candidate to be seen running around with some babe, having a great time while his opponent is out on the hustings."

Jennifer was so taken aback by his audaciousness

she nearly gasped. Quickly she said, "Next time you call me I'm calling Karen McAvoy." She added "hot stuff," and hung up.

She threw her head back in extreme annoyance. Bobby Bettman was merely a shark, a hired gun who'd attack anyone in the way of his candidate's victory. He was not typical of Ben's aides and associates.

Yet to Jennifer, Bobby represented an attitude shared by most members of Ben's staff and of the party people she'd met. Karen McAvoy, the campaign manager, was the exception; she seemed to like Jennifer immensely, as did Ben's nonpolitical friends. Karen warned Jennifer that she might incur subtle resentment from Ben's team since her controversial job made her a liability with some voters. And, of course, Jennifer had never stopped drawing scathing comments on other candidates endorsed by the party.

Just when she and Ben had thwarted any number of obstacles, new challenges cropped up like dandelions. Would their love truly overcome everything? She could only hope.

At the beginning of August Ben asked Jennifer if she'd like to accompany him on a week-long campaign swing through the state. "When we're done, you and I can spend a few days at my cabin on Lake of the Ozarks."

She happily accepted his offer and arranged for the time off. She wanted to share this vital part of Ben's life, even though she suspected she'd find campaigning very distasteful.

Ben helped her pack. "You'll need clothes that never wrinkle, plenty of deodorant, comfortable shoes, lots of Band-Aids, eyedrops—"

"Wait!" She guided him from her closet to a chair so she could snuggle in his lap. "What are the medical supplies for? In case the enemy opens fire on your caravan?"

"No, hon, the Band-Aids are for your adorable little feet," he responded, massaging her bare toes with one palm. "You'll be standing on them all the time. I want you to be as comfortable as possible, if not particularly glamorous."

Jennifer was impressed by the private jet, necessary for rapid statewide travel. It had all the comforts of home, and more: recessed lighting, wood-engrained fold-up tables, a small bar, sound system and fold-down limousine seats suitable for sleeping. She enjoyed the excitement of the thundering takeoffs and smooth three-point landings, the connections with helicopters and roomy vehicles.

The week was a blur of anonymous rural airports and county fairs and barbecues and district dinners, and at each event Jennifer saw for herself why Ben's political star had risen so high. His presence before a crowd was electrifying. He was an inspiring speaker, and of course he wrote all his own material. From all his outdoor speech making, his tan had become so deep that his eyes resembled light blue marbles. His summer suits looked as though they were pressed every hour, with him still in them. Representative Trostel seemed to exude power and glamour. No wonder he attracted women like nails to a magnet. As Jennifer stood unobtrusively among the people who milled around him she constantly heard women make remarks like "I wouldn't mind having his shoes under my bed!" She actually overheard two women directly proposition the candidate, unaware and surely uncaring, that his girlfriend was in the vicinity. Initially it disgusted her, but when she realized that passes must be made at Ben constantly, she was profoundly unsettled.

The couple's one stolen dinner à deux at a Kansas City restaurant was jarringly interrupted when a redhead slinked up to their table. With narrowed eyes she gave Ben a greeting that was simultaneously overly fond and icily hostile.

As she stalked away Jennifer pounced. "Did you have an affair with her, by any chance?"

"I'm not saying," Ben answered uncomfortably.

"You did, then."

In reply he covered one of her hands with his. His eyes were intent as he told her, "Darling, I promise I will never give you any reason to be jealous. Of course, you must do the same for me."

"I'll do my best." She tried to keep her lower lip from sliding out in petulance. This week was turning into a miserable ordeal, but she knew that was not Ben's fault directly.

As the week wore on, Jennifer observed the energy and vitality draining from Ben. He was an enthusiastic, people-loving campaigner, but the constant introductions, smiling, handshaking and autograph signing inevitably took their toll.

Various hangers-on, hoping to hitch a ride on a star, tended to remind Jennifer of vultures swarming over carrion. They fawned over Ben and contributed their counsel—against her, she often got the impression. Although a spirit of camaraderie prevailed on the plane, she was made to feel as welcome as a pile of dirty laundry, but Ben seemed unaware of her position. She was not a wife; thus, she guessed, she was considered an unknown and unpredictable quantity, a variable within political parameters. But she was not about to complain to Ben.

While Jennifer was bothered by the indifference of Ben's entourage, she was perversely fascinated by the carnival of the campaign process. It was affording her more insight for her political commentaries. She instructed herself, "Love the man, even if you hate his milieu." Yet her heart continuously asked her how much longer she could continue to admire completely a man whose closest associates she could not bring herself to respect.

The A-frame home on Lake of the Ozarks was clean, wonderfully secluded and heavily stocked with food and drink. The temperature was sweltering, but Jennifer basked in the feeling of the hot sun on her exposed skin. She and Ben ate and drank and slept and made love whenever they felt like it. They roamed the moss-green woods and rocky shores. Never had she known such romantic indolence and self-indulgence. She felt at peace there, at home with her future husband.

On the second evening the couple sat on chairs on their wooden dock, Ben poring over a position paper while Jennifer sipped lemonade and watched the sun set. The water reflected a neon glow. Birds called to each other. In the distance, motorboats purred over the lake. The hot, humid air was wrapped around them like a heavy blanket. Both Jennifer and Ben were dressed completely in white, like modish resort goers of the twenties.

Under cover of a wide-brimmed, straw hat Jennifer studied Ben's face, set in endearingly stern lines as he perused his paper. As she did so, the misgivings she'd been suppressing all week began to pound in her mind like a headache. Ben was the right man for her, the man she'd waited for all her life. But was *she* truly the right partner for him? She could hardly imagine a less apt senator's wife than herself.

She found the political limelight creepy, not glamorous. As Ben's wife she knew she would be unwilling and unable to represent him when he couldn't appear at events. She was dedicated to him but not to his political ambitions. She could not share him with the people on his staff, who constantly demanded more of his time, nor could she live with their mild enmity. And she certainly could not bear to watch predatory women paw Ben's well-tailored, well-maintained body!

Ben abruptly looked up at her, his eyes a violet flame in the twilight. "What are you looking at, girl?" he demanded mock roughly.

She was grave as she said, "Ben, I don't want to hurt your career."

He put down his reading and turned to her. "Now what does that mean?"

"I think that if I continue my cartooning after we marry, I'll be an embarrassment to you, not a credit."

"What brought all this on?"

"I love you, Ben. I'll never meet anyone else like you. I'm selfish, but I don't prefer success to love. That's why I'm willing to make some sacrifices when we marry."

"Such as?"

"Well, I'd stop doing the cartoons."

"No. There will be enough changes in your life with you leaving the *Herald* and moving to Washington."

"Maybe I could do a noncontroversial little comic

strip." She got the words out, but she looked as though she'd just swallowed cod liver oil.

"About anthropomorphic cats and puppies?" Ben guffawed and drew Jennifer within the circle of his strong arms. "I hardly think so! I couldn't be happy with a person who wasn't using her talents to their fullest. Think of how discontent you'd be. And how hard to live with!"

"Ben, I can follow my true calling in life or I can be lonely. I've been lonely long enough."

He shook his head. "Don't worry, hon. When we marry, everything will fall neatly into place." He stopped her further protests with a lengthy kiss that left her so dizzy her apprehensions fell away instantly. Drawing back from her, he urged, "Let's go for a swim."

Unhesitatingly, she let her white summer dress and hat drop to the planks at her feet. Their little cove, combined with the darkness of the early night, afforded them complete privacy. Drunk with the freedom of the moment, she plunged into the tepid, still water. Instantly she enjoyed the feeling of it over every millimeter of her skin.

She could see Ben's powerful shoulders and arms as he swam effortlessly toward the main part of the lake. He halted and treaded water while she caught up to him.

"Ben, w if a speedboat came roaring through here right now?" she demanded, breathing strenuously.

"You and I would die poetic deaths," he responded recklessly, splashing her.

They swam back toward the dock, romping and jumping around each other like two playful dolphins. Reaching shallower water where they could stand, Ben seized

Jennifer, pulled her hard to his slick, naked body and kissed her greedily.

The wetness and the dark made her feel as though they were elemental creatures of the night. Her passion rose like a ferocious summer storm, catching her by surprise.

They dragged themselves up onto the sand and Ben fell upon her body, his lips warm over the swollen, aching peaks of her breasts, his hands strong and sure over her flanks. He curved his palm lightly upon the lower part of her belly. She groaned and moved against him, wanton and demanding. Her breasts strained against the wet patch of his chest hair. When he moved his hand lower, she pressed into it, opening her thighs wide. She loved him so much she was unashamed of her own desire and needs. She trusted him. Then he was firm in her, and she felt his precious heat, his protectiveness and possessiveness.

She wanted the intimate moments to last forever, but the sweet agony was too much to bear. They kissed in the throes of their shattering release, a climax Jennifer felt throughout each and every one of her senses.

They lay on the damp sand, kissing lethargically as water lapped against the rocky shore. Jennifer's hands caressed Ben's body as though she could never get enough of him. As though she would never have him completely.

On their last day of leisure Jennifer and Ben went into the resort town of Bagnell, a typical tourist trap with its amusement parks and colorful attractions. By midafternoon her feet were sore and she was becoming hot and tired. She begged to sit for a moment.

"I've got a capital idea," Ben said. "You take a short rest while I go get us a couple of ice cream cones. They're the best antidote known for sore feet."

Jennifer nodded an eager agreement while sinking onto a white, gingerbread-trimmed bench. Her eyes followed his dashing figure adoringly. When he disappeared from view, she found herself suddenly gripped by some vague, misty pain. She fell into an unseeing trance as, uninvited, she recalled the specific problems that had bothered her that sultry night on Lake of the Ozarks. She could not stop pondering the differences and conflicts between them. The problems had been there since their first date, and this week on the campaign trail had only magnified them. Couldn't Ben see that for himself?

He had been engaged before, she thought, distantly hearing a group of children running noisily on the adjoining sidewalk. He knows so much can go wrong between two people even when they seem utterly committed to one another. He knows you've got to be practically *guaranteed* about your future together before you tie the knot.

We must decide how we're going to reconcile our professional incompatibility before we marry. And it's irreconcilable!

The enormity of their dilemma was being fully absorbed by her at last. A feeling of hopelessness clutched at her heart like a chill wind. Suddenly, she knew that when Ben became senator, their involvement must come to its end. She felt as if it were a life that must be sacrificed. Even if they extended all imaginable compromises toward each other, a senator could not be married to a poisonously skeptical political observer. In the end it all came down to that.

"They didn't have ice cream," came Ben's voice from behind her. "Is a snow cone all right?"

Jennifer was startled. Gathering her strength, she made her voice cheerful as she answered. "Snow cones! I love 'em."

Ben smiled and sat down to watch the casually clad tourists who walked on the path near them. He clearly mistook her quietness for lazy relaxation. His cooperative silence allowed Jennifer to strengthen, in her mind, her fierce decision. Eating the shaved ice without tasting its syrup, she told herself: you will continue with him till the general election. If he loses—and that would be the miracle he really doesn't want—then he can start the private career he's always been intended for, and you will marry. But when he wins, you have to vanish from his life. No marriage. No reunions. He will hate you, but you will have a collection of lovely, albeit bittersweet memories to cherish. Memories like precious jewels of the mind.

For now, she was going to grab all the wonderfully luminescent times with Ben that time would allow them. She would enjoy as much of the man she loved for as long as she could. She was ferociously determined to have the best time possible with Ben now.

She stood up energetically, crumpling the emptied paper snow-cone cup in one fist. "Well," she said with a puff of breath. "That was refreshing. What's next, honey?"

What was next was an observant young mother coming their way. She called to Ben as he stood up, "Say, Ben Trostel! You've sure got my vote for senator."

"Why, thank you," Ben replied, shaking her hand automatically. "It's always nice to meet a supporter."

"Do you want to kiss my baby for luck?" she asked merrily, hauling her infant from a stroller.

"I was just about to ask you if I could," he responded with a laugh. The woman giggled as if she were a teenager with a crush on Ben. Her babbling child was about nine months old and adorable, with blue eyes that rivaled Ben's in hue and luminescence. As he gathered the baby boy into his arms he held one of the tiny hands toward Jennifer.

"Look," he said tenderly, "did you ever notice how babies always look as though there's a tiny rubber band around their wrists because of their chubbiness?" He kissed the boy's cheek and bounced him up and down.

Jennifer was dumbstruck. The sweetness in Ben's nonchalant remark made her realize that he loved little children and doubtless wanted to be a father, something they'd never really discussed. She had desired children ever since she could remember, but she'd never allowed herself to think much about it as her biological time clock had ticked away.

She stared at him. With his eyes so blue and hers deep brown, their baby would be a genetic toss-up on eye color. How intriguing! But with a jolt, Jennifer reminded herself that this was a mystery she might never know the answer to.

"Jennifer, would you please return to planet Earth?" Ben said quizzically as he handed the baby back to its mother.

She said dully, "Just taking a walk into the future." He looked at her strangely, as if he did not recognize her.

Chapter Twelve

The call from the syndicate came the first day Jennifer was back at her *Herald* drawing board. "How soon can you begin churning out 'Hot Type'?" Mr. Agnelli asked.

He was referring to her proposed comic strip about a newspaper and its eccentric employees, and he said the syndicate wanted to distribute it as soon as possible.

"I can start immediately," she replied enthusiastically. After all, Ben's lengthy absences gave her plenty of time for this new project. And "Hot Type" was her ticket to commercial success.

"Your brand of wit is just as sharp as I had hoped, and the drawing style is fluid and forceful, just great!" Agnelli went on. "I'm sure some of our more conservative subscribers will prefer to print it on the editorial page, instead of the funnies page." He paused. "Say, is it true that you're dating a congressman who's running for the Senate?"

"Yes. Have you heard of Ben Trostel?" she asked with pride.

"Sure. He must be some catch. But what about conflict of interest?"

"I stopped doing cartoons about the Senate race a long time ago."

"Oh. Well, I imagine you can't go out with him after he gets into the Senate. If he makes it there, that is."

"Oh, he will," Jennifer replied shakily. Were all upper-level newspapermen like Agnelli and Frank Quarters so blunt and tactless? She couldn't stop herself from asking, "Why shouldn't we continue after he becomes senator?" She wanted his opinion.

"Are you kidding? In Washington, the 'democratic process' is accomplished mainly through the party circuit and networking. Not too many lawmakers would choose to socialize with the significant other of a political watchdog like yourself. You know that."

Jennifer's triumphant mood left her like a sigh. She switched the subject back to her new comic strip and felt deeply troubled for the rest of the day.

"I've decided *not* to mention you in that comprehensive profile I'm writing on Ben for the Sunday paper," Lynn said. She and Jennifer were meeting for the first time in weeks. With a start, Jennifer realized they were in the same restaurant where they had first discussed Ben.

"Oh thanks, Lynn, I'm so glad. What clinched your decision?"

"I know you enjoy as much privacy as you're permitted, and I always prefer to write about an interviewee's character without mentioning his or her romantic favorite, or favorites. I think people should stand on their own merits or drop on their own faults. The rest is all frosting I don't want to clutter my stories with."

"I like your reporting philosophy," Jennifer commented solemnly.

"I did a companion piece on Ben's opponent, too. Boy, he's no match for Old Blue Eyes, except in the fund-raising department. It's amazing that Ben is showing such a strong lead in the polls when you consider the other guy is in TV commercials and newspaper ads three to five times more often. Maybe he's doing so well because he's easier on the eyes than Williams is." Lynn winked lasciviously.

There was no levity in Jennifer's tone as she asked, "Lynn, do you really think Ben is going to be elected senator?"

"What?" Lynn made a scoffing noise. "Of course he is. After ten years of covering campaigns and candidates I've developed a surefire instinct for a winner. Believe you me, Ben practically glows with a senatorial halo already."

Suddenly Jennifer's eyes resembled two distress signals. "Lynn, if Ben wins the election I don't know what I'm going to do."

"What do you mean you don't know what you'll do?" she demanded, sensing real trouble.

"You're the first to know. Ben and I are supposed to get married after the election."

The reporter's eyes widened slightly but her face remained unreadable. "That seems... highly unlikely."

"I know." Jennifer wrung her hands. "Lynn, you're my good, wise friend. Tell me what *you* think."

"I'm not sure," Lynn began awkwardly, trying to be tactful. "Well, you're far too outspoken for one. Your work requires it, but in politics it's the kiss of death."

"You're absolutely right." Jennifer's dark eyes combed the room nervously. "I love Ben. I can't live without him . . . but I can't live in his particular environment. I can't shake hands and make polite conversation with every stranger I meet. I guess I . . . I think I don't *love* people as much as Ben does. Sure, I want to help society too, but in a different way." She looked desperately at Lynn. "I don't relish the 'roar of the crowd.' My forays into Ben's world of campaigns have made me feel like a criminal because I'm not Eleanor Roosevelt. When I'm around those people I think that there's something horribly wrong with me, that I'm some bitter, mistrustful skeptical bitch. How can I marry him, feeling this way? I don't enjoy the political arena. Love can't conquer that. And what would my controversial work do to Ben's career, his effectiveness and popularity?"

All the despair and anxiety she had harbored since her decision to disappear from Ben's life after his November victory were out at last. The effort of relating her troubles aloud left her drained. "So you see, Lynn," she added in a weaker, broken voice, "when Ben wins, I have to break off with him. We love each other, but we don't love each other's . . . community. The marriage would never work."

Her elbows propped on the table, Lynn nodded once. "How about if you gave up your cartooning?" she asked doubtfully.

"No. I once thought I could. But with my 'Hot Type' comic strip going into distribution soon, I've got the potential of being one of the hottest, most thought-provoking cartoonists in the country. No one in their right mind could give that up."

"And I'm sure Ben doesn't want you to."

"Ben's told me that to stop drawing would be to

betray my God-given ability. He says my talent can't be wasted."

Lynn placed her two cool hands on Jennifer's upper arms. "Have you two talked about all these issues?"

"Not to a great extent. Ben just tells me not to worry and if he isn't thinking about them, I don't want to bother him by bringing them up."

"He probably isn't talking because he probably isn't bothered by future problems that may not come to pass." Lynn paused before urging, *"Be* an unlikely senatorial wife, Jenny. Marry him."

"And single-handedly ruin his career?" Jennifer shook her head sadly and whispered, "I can't."

Lynn dropped her hands to her lap. "Speaking of careers, it's strange about Ben. . . ."

"What's strange?"

"Sometimes while I was interviewing him for this article, I got the feeling he wasn't nearly as hot and bothered about this race as his opponent is."

"I don't think he'd resort to dirty tricks to win it, if that's what you mean." Jennifer wasn't about to tell Lynn more. Ben's doubts were for her ears only and she knew Lynn was too good a reporter to let that kind of information pass. "Let's face it, he's got this race in the bag."

Summer glided into autumn, and the Senate race received more and more coverage in the local and national media. The stories often included a sentence to the effect of "the spirit of Harris Baker lives on in Ben Trostel." The persistent tie bothered the young congressman no end.

Jennifer was unbelievably busy preparing the first installments of "Hot Type" as well as keeping up with her daily cartoons, so she almost glad that Ben was gone so much of the time. A writer for the syndicate sent joke suggestions, leaving her free to concentrate on drawing the topical strip. At the same time she desperately wished she could spend every second of the day with Ben, for when he won the election, she knew there would be no more time for them.

In mid-October she went with Ben to the season's biggest fund raiser, a stuffy to-do held in the banquet room of the St. Louis Regency. Sitting at his side at the head table, Jennifer looked up at him proudly as he spoke. "We live in a complex, changing world, but never have there been such possibilities, such potential, in store for us. As Americans, we have more personal, intellectual and political freedom than ever before."

When he had finished speaking he bent over and for the fifth time told Jennifer how spectacular she looked. She'd invested in a cream-colored wool-sateen tuxedo jacket, which she wore with a bugle-beaded blouse. His compliment made her glow. Her curly hair was getting long and full, and it surrounded her animated face like a mink-colored cloud, throwing off little auburn highlights when she moved.

Ben tugged at her hand. "Come on," he said. "We're going to have a little fun."

"But I'm having fun now," she protested uselessly as Ben led her past dozens of round, linen-covered tables where people looked up from their five-hundred-dollar plates to gawk at the attactive young couple.

"No you're not," he said as they stepped onto the hotel terrace, high above the city. "I know you. These stuffy fund raisers aren't your scene." He kissed her temple, then put his arms around the front of her and rested his chin on the top of her head, so that they both faced the vista of St. Louis. The Gateway Arch gleamed darkly before them like a great scimitar.

"Some day, all this will be yours," Jennifer teased him.

"It already is," he answered without a trace of arrogance. "I'm congressional representative for this district, remember? And when we're married"—he chuckled—"I'll share it with you." He began rambling about suitable residences for them in St. Louis and Washington and when they'd make the official engagement announcement.

She responded to his talk with monosyllables, knowing he was only building castles in the air. Then he asked, "Will you be disappointed if I don't win?"

"How can you even suggest that, at this point?" she cried, turning to him. "Williams isn't running against you, he's running in place, according to all the surveys."

He shrugged, putting his hands on her shoulders. A mild breeze pushed a lock of her hair against her cheek. "You didn't answer my question."

"I'd be disappointed for you, Ben. I want you to have everything."

Her eyes sparkled with unshed tears. Did Ben really want to become senator? Even now? Did he honestly believe they could ever marry? Then he took her chin in his hand and gave her a kiss that made her forget where she was.

Jennifer leaped all over Ben when he arrived at her condominium late on the first Saturday night in November, kissing him and hugging him as though she'd never expected to see him again. As though she was never *expecting* to see him again.

"You always act like you're welcoming me home from the wars," he declared, swinging her joyfully by the waist.

"Or a puppy greeting its master coming home from work!"

"That, too," he said, and she struck him playfully on the shoulder. After several days of his absences, she always found herself startled anew by the blue intensity of his eyes. She could forget the extent of his handsomeness until he was right in front of her again. Tonight, though, his face looked a little gray and pinched, as though he were tired and worried beyond ordinary exhaustion.

"Well the last campaign trip is well and truly done," he announced, sinking onto the couch and dropping the Sunday morning paper beside him. "It's all over but the shouting—that is, the general election on Tuesday."

Though their eventual parting was a fact Jennifer could never forget, Ben's presence always charged her with radiant good spirits. She had learned to live with a certain constant depression, yet gloom seldom slipped over her when they were together. Tonight, however, she forced a false bravado that Ben would have perceived had he not been battle weary.

"Look at this," she said a little too brightly, seating herself next to him while holding up the top section of the newspaper. "The *Herald* poll says you're eleven points ahead of Walter B. Williams." Ben, looking at her Klee on the opposite wall, seemed not to have heard her. Saxophone music wailed softly from the stereo speakers. "Ben, doesn't that make you happy? You're going to be Missouri's next great senator!"

"If *you* start believing my campaign slogans, I don't know who to trust." He entangled some fingers in her dark curls. The slight smirk on his face was belied by the expressionlessness of his eyes.

"Darling, I must say you look rather . . . woebegone."

"I'm pretty fatigued, for one thing." He exhaled, stretched and looped one arm around her delicate shoulders. Reluctantly he confessed, "I don't know. I guess I'm experiencing some sort of anticlimax."

"You have put all your energy and time into this thing for six months. And then when you stand on the brink of success, and have nothing left to do, it's only normal that you're a little depressed."

Ben radiated a genuine smile and leaned over to kiss her uptilted nose lightly. "How did you ever get so smart, little girl?"

"My dad always told me, 'Be careful what you want, for you just may get it.'"

"Did your dad ever say that 'having is never the same as wanting'?"

"No. But I'll bet yours did."

Ben stopped joking and said, "Remember all the dissatisfactions about political life that I expressed to you that evening in Washington? It's when I'm tired like this that they stand out more than my love of the political and governmental processes. Then I wonder what a man so faint of heart is doing in this business."

Jennifer stared at him, opening and closing her lips. She could feel her hands trembling as she forced herself not to beseech him to quit, to drop the whole thing now, to run away to a place where they wouldn't have to see other people and be forced to make choices. Instead, she said dully, "It's not as though you're condemned to this life, Ben. You'll get your chance to write eventually."

"Yeah. After retirement." His expression changed from down-and-out to inspired. "I had a great idea for a book this week. What would you think of a former candidate's tell-all record of his campaigns? Nothing would be left out. The book would be both a critique and an exposé of the 'circus' aspects about politics that I abhor, but it would also be a guidebook of sorts for future campaigners. It could help other people avoid the mistakes I've made, and witnessed."

"It would be a surefire best-seller," Jennifer responded, sincerely impressed by the concept. "Campaign exposés have been written by reporters and aides, but never by a true insider. At least not one who could write well."

"Guess who'd do the cover art?" Ben said with a cunning smile.

Then the energy seemed to whisk out of his lanky frame again as he sighed. "But since I can't do it till I'm out of politics, I really don't know what the hell I'm talking about." His eyes took on a dull glaze.

Jennifer felt for him. Despite herself she countered, "Look at you, you've just spent another week on the road, being 'on' all the time, taking abuse while trying to make all kinds of people happy. How do you think you're supposed to feel? Tomorrow morning you'll have forgotten all about your depression, this feeling that you're stuck in a rut."

Ben tenderly regarded Jennifer's brave, lovely visage. "Of course this glumness is temporary. How can I ever feel sorry for myself when I've got you, sunshine?" He reached for her and gravely covered her mouth with his own. "Can you understand why I need you so much? Soon we'll be married, and then I'll truly have you. I will be absolutely, unrelentingly happy all of the time."

Staring at Ben as if she were trying to memorize all his features, she tried to keep her voice from cracking. "Ben ... I want you to hold me close ... very close."

There was a warm smile on his cowboy's face as he cradled her head between his large hands. He kissed her lovingly and deeply. Minutes passed, and their kisses and caresses became more insistently passionate. Then all was silent.

Later that night Jennifer sat up and gazed at Ben as he slept, fists curled alongside his face like a child's. Moonlight fell through the window in silver shafts, giving her lacy boudoir a bright mysterious shine.

Next week she would have to leave him for good. Surely he knew all the reasons for himself, and had known them as long as she had. After all, if she knew her career would taint and even ruin his own, and his entourage obviously knew it, he would not be in the dark.

Yet he was clearly unwilling to talk about the vital problem that polarized them. Perhaps, Jennifer thought suddenly, Ben had been fooling himself all along. She wished that she had the same capacity for illusion.

She tried to convince herself that she had done the right thing by not forcing the issue till Ben was senator. Then, in the flush of triumph, he would be ready to take the bad news, she assured herself, settling back against the cool cotton pillows.

She remained awake until dawn.

Chapter Thirteen

❧

The lengthy Lincoln came to a halt outside the condominium building. Jennifer emerged from the lobby wrapped in a black velvet evening cloak. She sniffed in the chill November air. There was a disturbingly damp, metallic quality to it.

Gracefully she edged inside the rear door of the spacious car, and Ben Trostel stretched his lanky body to give her a delightful sideways kiss. "Hello, beautiful," he said quietly. He burned a kiss into the soft palm of her hand. "I have something to give you later," he murmured so that the driver couldn't hear. She didn't allow herself to speculate on what that "something" might be.

Ben was wearing a simple charcoal-black business suit but he looked like a prince. It was the day of the general election, and a Senate seat was sure to be his within a matter of hours. The combination of his good looks and exhilarated victor's expression nearly took Jennifer's breath away.

She was amazed at how she could still feel a disturbing sexual attraction when she mournfully knew this was to be their last night together. Tonight, election night, was all politics, business and success for Ben. For Jennifer, the night was the beginning of a new era of aloneness. She couldn't even imagine the years ahead, sitting close to Ben as she was now, but she knew they lay in wait for her. It was time to face stark reality. When he won, she would lose.

Ben had just been driven in from the airport. The jet had carried him back from victory parties in Jefferson City and Kansas City, where he'd thanked and rallied his supporters. Missouri's polls had closed an hour before, at eight o'clock. They were now on their way to the party's chief victory celebration at the posh ballroom of the St. Louis Carleton Hotel bordering the Mississippi.

"Who did you vote for?" Ben asked conversationally, cradling Jennifer in his arms.

"You, of course." She didn't bother to mention the horrible stomach lurch she'd experienced as she pulled the lever for Trostel. "Who did you vote for?"

"Everyone in my party. Straight ticket." He was gazing happily out the front window.

"That means you voted for yourself."

"Sure. I had to vote for the candidate I believe in. Not for some name-calling business exec who's trying to *buy* the seat." There was no real rancor in his voice when he spoke of big-spending Walter B. Williams, though there should have been.

"I read today that with the money Williams has spent on this campaign, he could buy each one of the state's voters a TV set."

"Black and white or color?"

"I don't know," Jennifer said with a chuckle.

The Lincoln slowed as it neared the river and met the syrup-slow crawl of the traffic jam near the hotel.

The main drive to the Carleton entrance was blocked by network and local television vans. Well-dressed pedestrians were everywhere, either going into the hotel or leaving for other parties.

Jennifer pointed out, "Y'know, voting for yourself is dangerous business."

"What do you mean?" Ben should have been distracted looking out the window for acquaintances to glad-hand, familiar faces to wave at. But at the moment his heart and mind were concentrated on her.

"I did it once, and it turned out to be the most embarrassing thing I've ever done. When I was in fifth grade I ran for class secretary. I thought everyone liked my opponent Dickie Moore better, and that no one would vote for me. Thinking I needed every ballot I could get, I voted for myself. When the ballots were tallied, it turned out every single kid in the class had voted for Jennifer Aldrich. Except for one. When that ballot was marked off, I jumped up and yelled excitedly, 'That was mine!' "

"Oh no, you lied!" The crowd outside their windows was getting thicker as the car got closer to the hotel.

"But no one ever discovered my cowardly little lie," Jennifer went on, "because—"

The door on Ben's side of the car was pulled open by someone outside and his hand lost its grip on Jennifer's. An anonymous swarm jerked him effortlessly outside the Lincoln while he protested and laughed at the same time.

"Because Dickie Moore had also voted for himself," Jennifer finished aloud to herself in a dazed voice.

Voices chanted, "Trostel! Trostel! Trostel!" as fervently as though Ben were Charles Lindbergh returning from his 1927 flight across the Atlantic. She had a final glimpse of his back before the shouting throng enveloped him like a hungry amoeba. How was she ever going to find him in this mob?

She rubbed her forehead with her fingertips, muttering, "The evening is off to a bad start." In a louder voice she told the driver, "I'll get out here too." Feeling a little lost, she blindly fought her way through the masses of people to the Carleton's main door. Inside, there were more masses she had to work her way through, people laughing noisily, talking and arguing zealously, others watching, waiting, all clutching plastic cups of some alcoholic drink. Most wore tags identifying themselves. Many people there were quite important, others considered themselves to be.

Jennifer checked her cloak and cursed herself for wearing a suit. It was very becoming—long, lean, in a black and white check, with a stock-tied shirt—but it was far too warm. The swarm of party regulars and the television lights made the grand ballroom seem like a crowded sauna.

Someone tapped her on the shoulder, and she turned sharply to face a freckle-faced young woman. Like many people here tonight, she wore a blue "I've Got a Yen For Ben" button on her demure turtleneck.

"Excuse me," she asked politely, "but are you Ben Trostel's girl friend?"

Jennifer started proudly, "Well, I guess you could call me—"

The hateful words emerged from between clenched teeth. "Eat lead."

Instantly the woman vanished back into the crowd. Jennifer reeled. A psychopath, the raw material of an assassin! Politics had more than its share of loonies.

She was shaking her head in dismay when a comforting arm slid around her shoulders and the familiar voice said, "Don't tell me, Dickie Moore voted for himself too, right?" Jennifer was so happy to see Ben she could only gaze at him with relieved adoration. Ben added, "I thought I'd lost you forever out there."

A television camerawoman with a videopack strapped over one shoulder bumped the device into Jennifer's pelvic bone, and it hurt. Before she knew it, she had said the words that were mere wishful thinking. "You're stuck with me, hon."

They shared a secret moment there in the midst of that crazy room, holding each other silently.

Then a volunteer nearby hollered, "The first returns are in!"

The announcement was picked up and carried around the huge room. Every individual simultaneously turned to look at one of a dozen television sets, turned to a variety of stations. The colored numbers on every screen showed that with just a few precincts in Ben Trostel was running way ahead of Walter B. Williams.

Jennifer felt her heart drop to her feet. At the same time a cry went up. Again Ben was urged away from her to the stage, where he mumbled some pleased words.

Karen McAvoy came up to her, looking gorgeous in a column of crimson silk satin. "Jennifer, aren't you thrilled?" she said in that sultry voice Jennifer would never forget after the disastrous phone call.

Jennifer placed her hands at Karen's shoulders and answered indirectly, "You must be very happy tonight. You've done a marvelous job. And look at the results—a clear lead this early in the night!"

Karen gave a modest grin. "Those were just some urban precincts. The true test is yet to come. But between you and me, I think Ben may as well start planning his move into a Senate office building. Excuse me, but I see a very generous tycoon over there whom I must thank for the umpteenth time."

The blond campaign manager moved on. A dozen yards away Jennifer spotted the top of Ben's head. She needed him and was about to step in his direction when she saw a potbellied man next to her drop his lit cigarette and then grind it viciously into the thick ballroom carpet.

"Why did you do that?" she demanded of the stranger.

He shrugged. "We're in power, after all." Apparently he was referring to his political party.

Appalled, Jennifer couldn't think of a retort. "Your head is too big for your toupee, fella," she said finally before stalking off. She practically smacked into Lynn Fantle-Johnson, looking crisp and cool-looking in a linen dress and with notebook in hand. She seemed to be an island of calm within the raging sea of chaos.

"Have you seen the latest returns?" Lynn asked. "It's a close race, but Ben is leading in every precinct."

Jennifer's eyes filled with liquid, but she held back the tears. "I never thought I'd say this out loud, but I wish Ben were *trailing* in every precinct."

Lynn placed a palm on Jennifer's back and firmly steered her to a deserted alcove where they sat down. "You're really committed, aren't you? To not marrying that wonderful man if he wins."

Before Jennifer could utter another syllable, Bobby Bettman emerged from the crowd and was upon them. "Lynn! Jenny! How nice it is to see your happy, smiling faces!" He gave Lynn an outmoded "black power" handshake to which she returned a wan smile. To

Jennifer he said, "Guess I can start lobbying with your best guy for a Washington job now, eh Jenny?"

Fortunately, at that moment, Bobby was collared by an elderly gentleman who began reciting his victory in a soil-conservation district election several decades ago. The state party chairman announced that Governor Jacobson had just been reelected. His volunteers made strident war whoops. On the other side of the room a small band launched into a loud version of "Happy Days Are Here Again."

In the alcove Lynn and Jennifer enjoyed a pocket of quiet. Lynn now admitted, "I guess you *were* serious that day at lunch when you told me you planned to break it off. I'm beginning to understand your reasons, after overhearing your little exchange with the fat cat who was using the floor as the world's largest ashtray. I was right behind you."

"What do you mean?"

"That ugly turkey happens to be one of the richest men in the state, Jenny. He's given thousands to Ben's campaign. You simply can't antagonize contributors. They're mother's milk to politicians. If that guy knew your significance to Ben . . ." Lynn stopped and made a cutting gesture across her throat with one long, slender finger.

"You're right about my outspokenness, Lynn." Jennifer couldn't keep back a halfheartedly wry grin. "You can see that if I became Mrs. Senator Trostel, I'd separate Ben from his allies in no time flat. I simply can't shut myself up. Nor my pen." Her gaze traveled to the swaying, bobbing mass of humanity that began just a few feet from her chair, then back to Lynn. "To me, that contributor epitomized the majority of people who make politics their avocation—eager to attach themselves to anything they imagine as power, so they can believe in their own superiority."

"Is that how you honestly feel about politics and the people who participate in the electoral process?"

Lynn's question, and the way she posed it, were so searing that Jennifer was momentarily taken aback. But then she admitted her position with a nod.

"And you still haven't discussed this with the future senator?"

Jennifer felt hot and clammy. Her hair seemed to be dangling around her face like limp twine. "Not really," she replied. "I told you. He appears to want to believe I'd never be a liability to his position."

"He's wrong," Lynn admitted flatly. "But I guess I have to say that for now, with your attitude, your character, and your profession, you're bound to damage his career by going through with marriage. I care for the two of you dearly, but I must give my impartial, objective opinion."

A male voice boomed over the speakers. "Representative Benjamin Trostel is running ahead of Walter B. Williams by a margin of two to one in Missouri's metropolitan counties!"

Another shout went up, as though they were watching a bullfight. Lynn jumped up and shook hands with Ben, who had magically made a path to the alcove. Five or six party regulars were surrounding him like a bodyguard. As always, a loving warmth shot through Jennifer when his remarkable blue eyes settled on her. Distantly she could hear the whispered phrases of people scattered around them: "Jennifer Aldrich . . . political cartoonist . . ."

Ben leaned over her, his body radiating the only welcome heat in the place. The look on his face was tender. His eyes traveled over her features slowly, lovingly.

"Come up to the podium with me, Jennifer. It's time for me to introduce my sunshine at large."

She balked. "No Ben, this is your hour! Not yet—I'm too—"

"Too shy? Whatever you say." His expression was full of disappointment. Their gaze locked. Her heart pounded like a tiny hammer.

Behind him the TV screens flashed more voting figures, county by county. Several volunteers, picking and plucking at Ben, begged his presence on the stage again. He continued looking yearningly at Jennifer while he was pulled away from her as gradually as if he were in a slow-motion football replay. The tall figure melted in with the others till she could see no more of him. He was far, far away from her.

Jennifer seemed to wake up as if she'd been in a trance. She whipped her head from side to side, searching. Lynn was gone; she had reporting work to do. She was alone.

A swelling wave of applause and cheers accompanied Ben as he stepped next to Senator Dorothy Baker at the microphone. They were half-a-football field away from where Jennifer stood with her hands clasped and a wistful look on her small face.

All noise hushed as the gray-haired widow leaned on the podium. Her assured voice echoed across the room. "Ladies and gentleman of the party, how I wish my Harris were here to see Missouri's next great senator! Even Harris Baker himself never took all the metropolitan areas as quickly as our Benjamin Trostel has tonight!" As she gave Ben a possessive, somewhat stagy hug of congratulations, the crowd roared its approval and triumph.

Ben stepped to the microphone and humbly began, "We can't claim victory till a larger percentage of the ballots come in, but I must say this is a happy occasion."

Even from her corner Jennifer sensed her lover's fire and music. Very tall, handsome, charismatic—he was magnificent.

Yet she was not of his realm. She did not deserve him, she should not have him. Right here, in the ballroom, in the midst of his hour of triumph, she was a stranger in a strange land. The thick smoke, the laughter, the hot, perspiring clusters of bodies were suffocating her. She did not belong here. She never, never had.

Her mind flamed and she acted on impulse. She pivoted and headed for the coatroom, pushing recklessly through the smiling crowds. Just as her cloak was handed to her, she was tapped on the shoulder by Karen McAvoy.

"Jenny," she began, her beautiful face puckered with concern, "aren't you going to stay? Aren't you enjoying yourself?"

"Karen, could you do me a favor and tell Ben I didn't feel well?" That much was true. "It's an important evening for him, and I don't want to put a damper on it."

Loud, brassy music pounded in from the main room. Karen protested over the noise, "The night's not over yet! Only forty percent of the votes have been totaled." Her hazel eyes looked deeply, almost frantically into Jennifer's own. Then her face relaxed as she suddenly relented. "All right. We'll see you tomorrow, then."

Groups of people were trickling out of the Carleton

in a steady stream. The party was tapering off. The governor's seat had been retained, and senatorial victory was ensured. Jennifer moved past them quickly, a huddled figure in black. She turned down several offers from cabbies. She wanted to walk.

Two blocks from the hotel the streets resumed their usual postmidnight emptiness. Jennifer's heels hit the sidewalk in a staccato rhythm as she strode briskly toward her building, breathing in the cold morning air.

The zero hour had arrived all too quickly. It was over. Her time with the only man she had ever loved was over.

Two cars passed near her, one nearly sideswiping the other. Its horn shrilled with a sound of desperation. Jennifer felt it in her bones. Then the street was vacant again.

She stared fixedly, yet blindly, at the sidewalk between her toes. I cannot live without him, his giving love, his lovemaking; she repeated the words in her head like a litany. Why couldn't they be two other people, with two simpler lives? Then they could be together forever.

It was hopeless. She would always grieve for this one thing she and Ben could never have. Always. Yet she could never regret their love, and the warm, fulfilling moments it had given her.

It was two o'clock when she reached her apartment. The phone started ringing as she hung up the cloak. It sounded six times before stopping. That would be Ben—he knew it took a maximum of six rings for her to reach the telephone.

Jennifer took the receiver off the hook and went to bed.

* * *

She dozed fitfully, her dreams full of a senator she could not have. At four o'clock she rose to get some water. As she fumbled for a glass she heard the thump of the morning *Herald* landing against her front door.

Jennifer opened the door as if she were about to admit the plague. Quickly she picked up the paper, and as she had expected, the *Herald*'s headline proclaimed what she already knew: TROSTEL DEFEATS WILLIAMS. Other stories on the front page reported on state legislative and congressional races. Jennifer ignored them as her eyes combed the first paragraph on the senatorial contest, under Lynn's by-line:

"U.S. Senate candidate Benjamin Trostel seemed set Tuesday for general election victory over Walter B. Williams, the St. Joseph–based chief executive officer of Williams, Inc. Trostel consistently maintained a healthy lead over Williams last night with results tabulated from fifty-five percent of all precincts reporting."

Jennifer flung her water glass against the wall. She was shocked by her own craziness even before it landed.

When it did, it rolled to the ground with an empty "thunk." The glass was perfectly, infuriatingly intact. It was made of plastic.

Chapter Fourteen

Trying to sleep was useless. Jennifer put on a pair of jeans and a button-down shirt, then started some coffee before sitting down at the drawing board in her miniscule den. She tried to concentrate on sketching her "Hot Type" characters, but as her hand moved, her mind returned again and again on one fact: her relationship with Ben was over.

At five-thirty A.M. she replaced the phone headset in its cradle. She kept looking at the wall clock, whose hands seemed to be dragging around the face. She speculated on what Ben was doing at that moment and began to feel rather sheepish about stalking out of the victory party so dramatically.

At seven minutes after six, she heard the knock. She knew it was Ben. She rushed to the door and flung it open.

He stood at the threshold, winter coat draped over slumped shoulders. His face was haggard and drawn, his eyes bloodshot, his mouth a tired line.

Some things don't need to be spoken. The second she looked into his face, she realized that he'd sensed every one of her misgivings, that he knew why she'd left early last night and taken the phone off the hook. And that since he understood everything, he forgave her everything. His love was all-encompassing.

He looked as if he had been reported missing and presumed dead in some Central American war but managed to stagger back over the miles to her waiting arms. As they stood gazing at one another she suddenly realized—understood surely in a way she would never be able to explain—that he had lost the race. He was hers; they were free to be together. There would be no more problems, and no more fear.

He closed the door behind him and without a word they fell into each other's arms. They kissed carefully, slowly savoring what felt like the first, sweet touch of one another.

Finally Jennifer spoke, resting her head against his chest. "Ben, why aren't you at the hotel with your supporters?"

His voice had a brooding deepness. "Because I wanted to be alone with you. Because I couldn't bear sitting at the hotel any longer and hearing the returns come in. Other politicians wait for the final totals with their families, and you are my family, hon."

She pulled away to look at his face. Yes, he was losing. Her intuition was correct. She picked up the morning paper. "But according to this, you've already won."

"That's the early edition." He led her over to the couch. He turned on her television set and settled down with her on the suede couch. "My opponent has the edge as of this minute. We were running neck and neck just an hour ago, and now he's gaining on me."

Jennifer's huge brown eyes blinked once. "How can that be?"

Ben shook his head with a rueful smile. "Williams has heavy support in the rural areas of the state, Jennifer. Now those ballots are being tallied, and they're overtaking the urban ballots very quickly."

She stared at him. Ben was losing, though he'd worked relentlessly to earn the office. He was not going to be senator and he would no longer be congressman. Yet he was calm; he was tired, but he didn't seem devastated. She'd never seen a greater example of grace under pressure.

With a jolt, Jennifer realized that, in a way, she had won more of an upset victory than Ben's opponent had. But inside her there was a strange lump, an emotional space that sympathized for Ben in his defeat.

She distantly heard the local TV anchorman's tinny voice. "This is the closest general election Missouri has seen in decades, so close no one's going to call it for Trostel or Williams till nearly all of the state's precincts have reported. Williams currently has a narrow edge."

Ben chuckled uneasily. "See, babe? I might make a state history textbook or two with this race." At his bidding Jennifer settled into the crook of his arm. "And, looking at the silver lining, I may get to start my writing career now, instead of God knows when."

The exhausted-looking anchorman announced, "With us in the studio we have Frank Quarters, editorial editor of the St. Louis *Herald*." Jennifer was mildly surprised to see her own boss, bow tie and all, sitting on the news panel as a commentator. "Walter B. Williams is pulling one percentage point ahead of Representative Trostel. Last Sunday the *Herald*'s polls indicated that Trostel had an eleven-point spread over Williams. Frank, what went wrong there?"

Quarters glared into the camera. "The polling firm that the *Herald* uses for its election surveys is unusually accurate in its methods and predictions. Yet every once in a while this sort of firm blows it. It looks like our pollsters finally called one wrong. And in spades! Not only did they call it wrong, but—"

The anchorman, as well as his audience, could tell the editor was about to let loose with a blistering curse. Quickly he asked, "Frank, this morning's first edition of the *Herald* stated that Trostel won his race. This brings to mind Harry Truman's 1948 victory, which had the papers announcing DEWEY DEFEATS TRUMAN. How did this happen?"

This time Quarters appeared ready to leap out of his skin with anger at himself and his colleagues. "Our premature declaration resulted from our failure to recognize the heavy backing that Williams received from Missouri's farmers and small-business owners. With sixty percent of the precincts reporting, the *Herald* agreed with the wire services that Trostel's lead was so big it wasn't going to be overcome."

Then Frank barked, "After all, we're only a newspaper. We just get the facts and print them by deadline."

Ben and Jennifer couldn't help but laugh merrily at Quarters' snarled protest despite the sourness of the occasion. Then Ben soberly stated, "It looks as though there'll be no more career conflict for us, Sunshine. If I had won . . ."

Jennifer smiled sadly and gently touched Ben's face. "It's not over yet."

"Sshhh. Listen to me. If I had won, we would have had to reanalyze our plans. So let's look at the bright side. My defeat has put one problem to rest." He smirked humorlessly. "Perhaps many problems. We can't forget the fact that I was often fed up with public life. Now I can have a private career and have my time to myself. To ourselves."

"You haven't forgotten your book concept, have you?"

"Are you kidding?" He patted his lapel pocket, where Jennifer knew he always kept a small leather memo book. "I started taking notes as soon as I hatched the idea."

On the TV, it was announced that Williams had increased his lead to nearly one and a half points. Jennifer gazed at Ben lovingly. Though in her heart she felt anguish for him, for his apparent loss, there was a warm feeling in the core of it. For now she knew that win or lose, everything would have been all right between her and Ben. Her long-standing fears had been overinflated, and selfish, all along. Her melancholy ruminations had been remarkably unthinking.

"I'm so sorry, darling," she said. "You are the best man. You should have won." She started to put her arms around Ben, but he stood up.

He was dry-eyed and resolute. "Thanks, Jennifer. I'm going to hop in the shower, if you don't mind. I want to look clean and confident as hell for that concession speech."

Jennifer dozed on the couch while he showered. When she woke, she saw him sitting next to her, one hand laid on her calf, his high-voltage eyes fixed on the set. His suit was fully renewed and his hair was damp from the shower. He looked dignified and, the only other adjective Jennifer could think of was, "senatorial."

She heard the voice from the television. "We believe we have the final results now in the U.S. Senate race between Walter B. Williams and Benjamin Trostel. In the closest race we've ever seen, Williams has defeated Trostel by a margin of just under two percent."

Then Frank Quarters' authoritative voice: "It's one of the biggest upsets I've ever seen. This just wasn't Trostel's year. For one thing, many consider him too young to be running for the Senate. He's not quite right for the current voter profile this season. Actually, I consider his opponent's advertising blitz to have been the major factor—"

Ben hit the power button, plunging the room into abrupt silence. He moved to the window and looked out toward the Mississippi for a minute. When he turned back to Jennifer he wore a long, full grin.

"Come on, Jennifer. Put on a pretty dress and let's go thank the wise folks who gave me their votes. And show the others what fools they were to vote me down."

Tears dimmed Jennifer's rounded eyes. "Ben, how are you feeling? Tell me, really."

He spoke with a composure that made her proud. "I'd be lying if I didn't say I'm a little confused right now, baby. Naturally I'm disappointed, I'm regretful. But I'm also extremely relieved. I'm surprised how relieved I feel! Now I can assume a private life, and we can start a marriage away from the limelight. My enduring commitment to you cuts right through all the confusion I'm feeling. Whenever I think back to my bid for the Senate, you are the best thing I'll remember. So overall, darling, I am very, very happy." By now he was back up to his full level of self-assurance. He was as purposeful, fearless and gallant as Jennifer had ever seen him.

Suddenly he clutched at the inside pocket in his jacket. "My god, I forgot! I don't see how . . . or maybe

I do . . ." With an elegant flourish he withdrew a very small blue velvet box and presented it to Jennifer. She looked at him solemnly as she opened the box, then gasped at the fiery emerald-cut diamond that was nestled inside. She gasped, then gasped again. The top layer of her skin felt frozen with joy.

Ben seemed amused by her ecstatic confoundment. With his fingertips he brushed aside the curls at her forehead before taking back the velvet box. He then withdrew the ring and slid it over the third finger of her left hand. Still Jennifer was speechless.

"What's the matter? Don't you like it? The jeweler said I could take it back . . ."

Typical masculine puzzlement, Jennifer noted as she stroked the cold stone over her silky cheek. How was she to explain to Ben what this ring signified to her? This solitaire was nothing less than a prophecy of many shared seasons to come, a hard-won guarantee that they'd be together eternally.

Collecting herself, she stood and looped her arms around his strong neck and kissed him lingeringly. "Like it? Honey, I love this ring. I already cherish it." In a slow whisper she declared, "I love you, Ben. I always will. That's what your ring means to me."

He looked immensely pleased with himself. He lovingly studied her shining visage, then hugged her so that she was lifted bodily off the floor. "Jennifer, honey, I'll love you always." His voice sounded like it was basking in a buttery contentment. "If only you knew how happy you make me."

He set her down, the two of them still pressing closely along the lengths of their upright bodies. He kissed her sweetly on the end of her uptilted nose, then stated practically, "We must make plans."

"Wedding plans?" Jennifer returned excitedly.

"Well, those too. But first we've got to plan just how we're going to let everyone else in on our secret. . . ."

Camera flashes erupted as Ben and Jennifer mounted the stage of the Carleton Hotel ballroom. That morning the room was still warm but not nearly as sweltering as it had been at midnight. Reporters, photographers and Ben's most loyal supporters stood in scattered groups within the cavernous space.

After a number of staffers and journalists had shaken his hand, Ben stepped to the microphone. Looking every inch a winner, he launched into a well-spirited concession speech.

Jennifer stood at his side, wearing an emerald-green velvet coat-dress with a doily-lace collar. One hand was linked surreptitiously with Ben's behind the podium. Her white face was solemn, but her eyes shimmered with barely suppressed emotion.

"I've greatly enjoyed my public career, and my opportunity to serve others," Ben stated in a clear, ringing voice. "I leave office very content, and at peace. My life has been enhanced immeasurably by those talented, honorable people I've been privileged to meet."

If one looked closely at Jennifer, it was impossible not to see the ring on her left hand. The sizable solitaire diamond there shone like a star.

"I lost a lot this morning, but I've won a lot too," Ben continued happily, drawing Jennifer close to the podium. The expression on his face told his secret for him.

Jennifer Trostel stretched indolently in the double bed, extending her limbs as far as they could go. One hand smoothed against the bare, golden back of her husband, who stirred without waking. She smiled without being aware of it and possessively glanced at the rings on her left hand.

Without disturbing Ben, she slid off the bed and went to look out the window. A flurry of early-winter snow was falling in brittle white flakes over the Potomac and Virginia. The morning's creamy light washed shadows over her body as she stood, naked but very warm. Healthy sensuality seemed to ooze right out of her pores. Her very skin glowed with happiness and desire.

The last two weeks since the election had passed as quickly as if she had been ripping pages off a calendar.

If anything, the election defeat had only made Ben better-looking. He did not make it clear to the media whether he was going to completely retire from public life. All he told them was, "I'm relatively young. I intend to return to public service in some capacity, but not in the near future."

Actually, the news of his engagement to Jennifer had upstaged his loss. Not only was "Glamour Boy" Trostel, one of Missouri's most eligible bachelors, finally tying the knot, he was also wedding the *Herald*'s lively young political cartoonist. Jennifer Aldrich was attractive, but she belonged to the last profession in the world a politician would be expected to marry into, according to the consensus of local press gossip.

Lynn Fantle-Johnson's reportorial cool finally broke, and she begged for an exclusive interview with the most glamorous and intriguing couple in St. Louis. Jennifer's abhorrence of publicity broke down, and she gushed for the record, "I'm in love with this person, and marriage is a way of letting the entire world in on the fact. So we're going through with the nuptials as soon as we can."

There had been a bright whirl of engagement parties for the couple; the small chapel wedding (where both Jennifer's and Ben's mothers wept copiously, overjoyed to see their bachelor children wed at last); then the announcement that the president was calling a special lame-duck session of Congress.

Three days after the wedding, the newlyweds had returned to Washington, where part of their honeymoon would be spent packing up Ben's belongings. They were discussing the purchase of a home outside downtown St. Louis. Jennifer decided to hold down her cartooning slot at the *Herald* until she was certain of "Hot Type's" success on the funny pages.

"Honey—"

Jennifer turned around. Ben was sitting up in bed, exposing the upper half of his body.

"Don't you think somebody's going to see you standing there without a stitch on?" His eyes looked blue enough to swan dive into. He opened his arms in silent invitation.

"Only if they've got binoculars!" She jumped into the fragrant shelter of his hard torso. Her hair brushed her white shoulders. "The view," she said, pausing to kiss the end of his finely carved nose, "is just for your eyes." Ben's hands glided up to cup the soft weight of her breasts. Instantly she slid into the spell of desire. The stem of her slender neck leaned back as his head moved downward.

The phone rang and the couple pulled apart. They looked at each other and sighed regretfully. The mood was broken. Reluctantly Ben picked up the receiver, simultaneously enclosing Jennifer under one arm. She adoringly watched his face as he talked animatedly.

"Good morning. Hi, Governor!" With a start Jennifer realized that the governor of Missouri had just interrupted the Trostels' bout of conjugal bliss. It would still take time for her to get used to the caliber of people Ben counted among his associates. Ben listened to the Jefferson City–based voice for some time, one of his hands tangling playfully in her long, dark curls.

"I can't thank you enough, sir, I'm very honored, but I really can't accept that offer, I can tell you that right now," he said after a while, polite but resolved. "Of course I'm considering offers from St. Louis law firms. And I got a pleasant surprise yesterday. A major publishing house in New York wants me to come up there next week. They've invited me to write a coffee-table biography of Harris Baker."

Ben chuckled expansively at something the governor said. "Don't tell anyone in the party, but this defeat is beginning to seem like the best thing that ever happened to Ben Trostel." His gaze zeroed in on Jennifer, and an effervescent affection spilled out of those azure eyes. "I'll tell her that, Governor. I'll use my best influence to make her go lighter on you, but I think it's a lost cause."

He hung up the phone and put both arms around Jennifer. "What did he offer you?" she asked.

"He wanted me to be a state commissioner."

"With all that self-aggrandizing information you were giving the guv, why didn't you also throw in the fact that you want to work on your marriage for a while?" she asked coyly, bringing one shoulder up toward her ear.

"Darling, we don't have to work on any marriage," Ben retorted lightly. "Let's face it, you and I have withstood all the tests and struggles any marriage could present."

"We shall see! One thing we don't lack is stamina, we've found that out." There was a querulous note in her response. "Ben ... you're going through so much—change of job, residences. I'm not sure I could withstand them, personally. How do *you* feel about all these changes?"

"Change? I love it! It's growth, it's improvement. From now on, everything is going to be so much better. Thanks to you, Jennifer, it seems like I'm finally living my life."

"No, darling. *We're* finally living *our* lives."

Their arms tightened around each other. Each looked into the other's eyes as though searching for something tangible. They found no more doubt, no more loneliness anywhere. Only the pure, scintillating flame of an emotion they were at last free to feel fully, without barriers, without ties to circumstance and situation. A golden flower of light bloomed in their eyes, to be seen only by those who knew it was there.

GET SIX RAPTURE ROMANCES EVERY MONTH FOR THE PRICE OF FIVE.

Subscribe to Rapture Romance and every month you'll get six new books for the price of five. That's an $11.70 value for just $9.75. We're so sure you'll love them, we'll give you 10 days to look them over at home. Then you can keep all six and pay for only five, or return the books and owe nothing.

To start you off, we'll send you four books absolutely FREE. "Apache Tears," "Love's Gilded Mask," "O'Hara's Woman," and "Love So Fearful." The total value of all four books is $7.80, but they're yours *free* even if you never buy another book.

So order Rapture Romances today. And prepare to meet a different breed of man.

YOUR FIRST 4 BOOKS ARE FREE! JUST PHONE 1-800-228-1888*

(Or mail the coupon below)
*In Nebraska call 1-800-642-8788

Rapture Romance, P.O. Box 996, Greens Farms, CT 06436

Please send me the 4 Rapture Romances described in this ad FREE and without obligation. Unless you hear from me after I receive them, send me 6 NEW Rapture Romances to preview each month. I understand that you will bill me for only 5 of them at $1.95 each (a total of $9.75) with no shipping, handling or other charges. I always get one book FREE every month. There is no minimum number of books I must buy, and I can cancel at any time. The first 4 FREE books are mine to keep even if I never buy another book.

Name	(please print)
Address	City
State	Zip	Signature (if under 18, parent or guardian must sign)

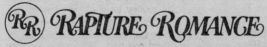

This offer, limited to one per household and not valid to present subscribers, expires June 30, 1984. Prices subject to change. Specific titles subject to availability. Allow a minimum of 4 weeks for delivery.

RR 183

RAPTURE ROMANCE

*Provocative and sensual,
passionate and tender—
the magic and mystery of love
in all its many guises*

Coming next month

A DISTANT LIGHT by Ellie Winslow. As suddenly as he'd once disappeared, Louis Dupierre reentered Tara's life. Was it the promise of ecstasy, or some unknown, darker reason that brought him back? Tara didn't know, nor was she sure whether she could risk loving—and trusting—Louis again . . .

PASSIONATE ENTERPRISE by Charlotte Wisely. Gwen Franklin's business sense surrendered to sensual pleasure in the arms of executive Kurt Jensen. But could Gwen keep working to prove she could rise as high as any man in the corporate world—when she was falling so deeply in love?

TORRENT OF LOVE by Marianna Essex. By day, architect Erin Kelly struggled against arrogant builder Alex Butler, but at night, their lovemaking was sheer ecstasy. Yet when their project ended, so did their affair, and Erin was struggling again—to make Alex see beyond business, into her heart . . .

LOVE'S JOURNEY HOME by Bree Thomas. Soap opera star Katherine Ransom was back home—and back in the arms of Joe Mercer, the man who'd once stolen her heart. But caught up in irresistible passion, Katherine soon found herself forced to choose between her glamorous career— and Joe . . .

AMBER DREAMS by Diana Morgan. Jenny Moffatt was determined to overcome Ryan Powers and his big money interests. But instead, his incredible attractiveness awed her, and she was swept away by desire . . .

WINTER FLAME by Deborah Benét. Darcy had vowed never to see Chason again. But now her ex-husband was back, conquering her with loving caresses. If Chason wanted to reestablish their marriage, would his love be enough to help her overcome the past. . . ?

RAPTURE ROMANCE

*Provocative and sensual,
passionate and tender—
the magic and mystery of love
in all its many guises*

NEW Titles Available Now

(0451)

#33 ☐ **APACHE TEARS by Marianne Clark.** Navajo Adam Hawk willingly taught Catriona Frazer his secrets of silversmithing while together they learned the art of love. But was their passion enough to overcome the prejudices of their different cultures? (125525—$1.95)*

#34 ☐ **AGAINST ALL ODDS by Leslie Morgan.** Editorial cartoonist Jennifer Aldrich scorned all politicians—before she met Ben Trostel. But love and politics didn't mix, and Jennifer had to choose which she wanted more: her job or Ben.... (122533—$1.95)*

#35 ☐ **UNTAMED DESIRE by Kasey Adams.** Lacy Barnett vowed ruthless land tycoon Ward Blaine would never possess her. But he wore down her resistance with the same gentleness and strength he used to saddle-break the proudest steed... until Lacy wasn't fighting his desire, but her own... (125541—$1.95)*

#36 ☐ **LOVE'S GILDED MASK by Francine Shore.** A painful divorce made Merilyn swear never again to let any man break through her defenses. Then she met Morgan Drake.... (122568—$1.95)*

#37 ☐ **O'HARA'S WOMAN by Katherine Ransom.** Grady O'Hara had long ago abandoned the high-powered executive life that Jennie Winters seemed to thrive on. Could she sacrifice her career for his love—and would she be happy if she did? (122576—$1.95)*

#38 ☐ **HEART ON TRIAL by Tricia Graves.** Janelle Taylor wasn't going to let anyone come between her and her law career. But her rival, attorney Blair Wynter, was equally determined to get his way opposite her in the courtroom—and the bedroom...
(122584—$1.95)*

*Price is $2.25 in Canada

To order, use coupon on next page

RAPTURE ROMANCE

*Provocative and sensual,
passionate and tender—
the magic and mystery of love
in all its many guises*

(0451)
- #19 ☐ CHANGE OF HEART by Joan Wolf. (124421—$1.95)*
- #20 ☐ EMERALD DREAMS by Diana Morgan. (124448—$1.95)*
- #21 ☐ MOONSLIDE by Estelle Edwards. (124456—$1.95)*
- #22 ☐ THE GOLDEN MAIDEN by Francine Shore. (124464—$1.95)*
- #23 ☐ MIDNIGHT EYES by Deborah Benét (124766—$1.95)*
- #24 ☐ DANCE OF DESIRE by Elizabeth Allison. (124774—$1.95)*
- #25 ☐ PAINTED SECRETS by Ellie Winslow. (124782—$1.95)*
- #26 ☐ STRANGERS WHO LOVE by Sharon Wagner. (124790—$1.95)*
- #27 ☐ FROSTFIRE by Jennifer Dale. (125061—$1.95)*
- #28 ☐ PRECIOUS POSSESSION by Kathryn Kent. (125088—$1.95)*
- #29 ☐ STARDUST AND DIAMONDS by JoAnn Robb. (125096—$1.95)*
- #30 ☐ HEART'S VICTORY by Laurel Chandler. (125118—$1.95)*
- #31 ☐ A SHARED LOVE by Elisa Stone. (125126—$1.95)*
- #32 ☐ FORBIDDEN JOY by Nina Coombs. (125134—$1.95)*

*Prices $2.25 in Canada

Buy them at your local

bookstore or use coupon

on next page for ordering.

RAPTURE ROMANCE

*Provocative and sensual,
passionate and tender—
the magic and mystery of love
in all its many guises*

(0451)
- # 1 ☐ LOVE SO FEARFUL by Nina Coombs. (120035—$1.95)*
- # 2 ☐ RIVER OF LOVE by Lisa McConnell. (120043—$1.95)*
- # 3 ☐ LOVER'S LAIR by Jeanette Ernest. (120051—$1.95)*
- # 4 ☐ WELCOME INTRUDER by Charlotte Wisely. (120078—$1.95)*
- # 5 ☐ CHESAPEAKE AUTUMN by Stephanie Richards. (120647—$1.95)*
- # 6 ☐ PASSION'S DOMAIN by Nina Coombs. (120655—$1.95)*
- # 7 ☐ TENDER RHAPSODY by Jennifer Dale. (122321—$1.95)*
- # 8 ☐ SUMMER STORM by Joan Wolf. (122348—$1.95)*
- # 9 ☐ CRYSTAL DREAMS by Diana Morgan. (121287—$1.95)*
- #10 ☐ THE WINE-DARK SEA by Ellie Winslow. (121295—$1.95)*
- #11 ☐ FLOWER OF DESIRE by Francine Shore. (122658—$1.95)*
- #12 ☐ DEAR DOUBTER by Jeanette Ernest. (122666—$1.95)*
- #13 ☐ SWEET PASSION'S SONG by Deborah Benét. (122968—$1.95)*
- #14 ☐ LOVE HAS NO PRIDE by Charlotte Wisely. (122976—$1.95)*
- #15 ☐ TREASURE OF LOVE by Laurel Chandler. (123794—$1.95)*
- #16 ☐ GOSSAMER MAGIC by Lisa St. John. (123808—$1.95)*
- #17 ☐ REMEMBER MY LOVE by Jennifer Dale. (123816—$1.95)*
- #18 ☐ SILKEN WEBS by Leslie Morgan. (123824—$1.95)*

*Price $2.25 in Canada

Buy them at your local bookstore or use this convenient coupon for ordering.
THE NEW AMERICAN LIBRARY, INC.,
P.O. Box 999, Bergenfield, New Jersey 07621
Please send me the books I have checked above. I am enclosing $_____
(please add $1.00 to this order to cover postage and handling). Send check or money order—no cash or C.O.D.'s. Prices and numbers are subject to change without notice.

Name_____

Address_____

City _____ State _____ Zip Code _____

Allow 4-6 weeks for delivery.
This offer is subject to withdrawal without notice.

SPECIAL $1.00 REBATE OFFER
WHEN YOU BUY
FOUR RAPTURE ROMANCES

To receive your cash refund, send:

1. This coupon: To qualify for the $1.00 refund, this coupon, completed with your name and address, must be used. (Certificate may not be reproduced)

2. Proof of purchase: Print, on the reverse side of this coupon, the *title* of the books, the *numbers* of the books (on the upper right hand of the front cover preceding the price), and the U.P.C. numbers (on the back covers) on your next four purchases.

3. Cash register receipts, with prices circled to:
   Rapture Romance $1.00 Refund Offer
   P.O. Box NB037
   El Paso, Texas 79977

Offer good only in the U.S. and Canada. Limit one refund/response per household for any group of four Rapture Romance titles. Void where prohibited, taxed or restricted. Allow 6–8 weeks for delivery. Offer expires March 31, 1984.

NAME_____

ADDRESS_____

CITY_____STATE_____ZIP_____

SPECIAL $1.00 REBATE OFFER
WHEN YOU BUY
FOUR RAPTURE ROMANCES

See complete details on reverse

1. Book Title _____

   Book Number 451-_____

   U.P.C. Number 7116200195-_____

2. Book Title _____

   Book Number 451-_____

   U.P.C. Number 7116200195-_____

3. Book Title _____

   Book Number 451-_____

   U.P.C. Number 7116200195-_____

4. Book Title _____

   Book Number 451-_____

   U.P.C. Number 7116200195-_____